Cain's Book

Cain's Book

Alexander Trocchi

Foreword by Greil Marcus
Introduction by Richard Seaver

Grove Press
New York

Published by Grove Press
A division of Grove Press, Inc.
841 Broadway
New York, NY 10003–4793

Library of Congress Cataloging-in-Publication Data

Trocchi, Alexander, 1925–1984
    Cain's book / Alexander Trocchi ; foreword by Greil Marcus ;
    introduction by Richard Seaver.
        p.   cm.
    ISBN 0-8021-3314-2 (acid-free paper)
    1. Trocchi, Alexander, 1925–   —Fiction. I. Title.
PR6070.R56C28   1992
823'.914—dc20   92-24900
                                                                      CIP

Manufactured in the United States of America

Printed on acid-free paper

First Edition 1960
First Evergreen Edition 1960
First Black Cat Edition 1961
Second Evergreen Edition 1992

10 9 8 7 6 5 4 3 2 1

For Lyn

Foreword

Alexander Trocchi was a legendary figure in his lifetime: "a Viking," as one who knew him in Paris in the 1950s recalled. He was seen as a man of towering literary genius, fated to cut a swath through the world. The only question was which direction he might choose. In the fifties he kept company with writers as austere as Beckett and with revolutionaries as shadowy as Guy Debord, as well as with hustlers straddling the line between art and crime. In the sixties he announced himself a "cosmonaut of inner space" and positioned himself at the center of an international combine of the avant-garde, the "underground," the "new culture"; with real force and passion he called for an "Invisible Insurrection of a Million Minds." Always—whether in Paris or London, New York or Venice, California—people of all sorts were powerfully drawn to him, to his keening vitality, to the promises of adventure, risk, and victory he seemed to scatter like gifts to those less rich in spirit—like alms to the poor.

But when Trocchi died in London in 1984—he was 59; he died of pneumonia, following an operation the previous year for lung cancer—he left behind a very conventional bohemian legend. He had been a heroin addict for almost thirty years, unrepentant and proud, and all around him was wreckage: his second wife, an addict in his steps, dead young, long before him (reaching the nadir of the bohemian cliché, Trocchi had once sent her out into the streets of Las Vegas to whore for their junk); his eldest son, dead; his youngest son, who would kill himself a few months after his father's death. Across the map of Trocchi's life were friends and acolytes who died young or who cultivated their own addictions. And, of course, there was the wreckage of Trocchi's own writing, almost all behind him by the end of the 1950s: from the pornography published in Paris under the name "Frances Lengel" to the lonely *Cain's Book*, an autobiographical novel in the form of a junkie's journal. *Cain's Book* was celebrated upon publication in 1960 in New York, banned and burned in Great Britain in 1963 as likely to corrupt and deprave. That was all. For the next quarter century Trocchi pursued a thousand schemes for a little money, a little notoriety, living off the question of what might have been. In the matrix of the bohemian legend there is nothing so romantic as turning one's back on the field the moment everyone believes the prize is yours; in that sense, in the sense of rules that were not of his making but for which he settled, Trocchi's life was a cheap triumph.

Cain's Book, written over the course of seven years, is not cheap. It is cruel. It is one of those nihilist books that well-meaning readers are always trying to rescue from itself with appeals to sociology, philosophy, art, or revolution. *The book provides valuable insights into the nature of a major social problem. . . . Beneath the surface the book affirms the irreducible nature of the human spirit. . . . The book makes a crucial contribution to the literature of addiction . . . of alienation . . . of rebellion*—forget it. You can't derive socially useful sentiments from lines like " 'She'd suck the fix out of your ass.' " There is no subversive undertow in a solipsistic rant like ". . . and set their damn police on me who has not stirred from this room for fifteen years except to cop shit. . . ." *Cain's Book* insists that life is made of choice and necessity, and then moves relentlessly toward reducing both elements to zero. "Sometimes, at low moments," says the narrator of *Cain's Book*, "I felt my thoughts were the ravings of a man out of his mind to have been placed in history at all, having to act, having to consider; a victim of the fixed insquint. Sometimes I thought: What a long distance history has taken me out of my way! And then I said: Let it go, let it go, let them all go!"

"I have needed drugs," read a note found among Trocchi's papers after his death, "to abolish within myself the painful reflection of the schizophrenia of my times, to quench the impulse to get at once onto my feet and go out into the world and live out some convenient, traditional identity of cunning and contriving. . . . The astronauts who were my heroes moved on trajectories of inner space. . . . I wanted to escape out of the prison of my mind's language; to 'make it new.'" Against such trite phrases about salvation through art, *Cain's Book* is an account of how drastically they fall short. "I'm all the time aware it's reality and not literature I'm engaged in. . . . At times I am living at the tips of my senses. I am near flesh, blood, hair." None of this is any good against the enemy that, near the end of the book, finally reveals itself: history, the rebuke of a world that would be no different were you never born, that is not waiting for you to die. "It is as though I have been writing hesitantly, against the tide, with the growing suspicion that what I have written is in some criminal sense against history. . . . "

Such bravado comes off the pages of *Cain's Book* as bluster; as a pathetic admission of defeat; as a distant memory of an idea of art as a subjective, solitary annihilation of a world which refuses to recognize the sound of its own ending, the sound the artist makes. *Cain's Book* builds directly to this silent explosion; you can hear it going off in the writer's head. This explosion is art in spite of itself. As you read, it is loud enough to silence the chatter of Trocchi's merely personal legends. Let them go.

Greil Marcus
1992

Introduction

In 1991 a young Scottish critic, aptly named Andrew Murray Scott, published a biography of Alexander Trocchi entitled *The Making of a Monster*. The book, though riddled with errors of fact and interpretation, nonetheless came as a shock. It reminded me forcibly that Trocchi, who when I first met him was as close to a definition of "life force" as I had ever encountered, was not only dead but virtually forgotten. The man whom William Burroughs had rightly touted as "a unique and pivotal figure in the literary world of the 1950s and 1960s" was, by the time of his death in 1984, hardly remembered even in his native Scotland.

The book was also a graphic shock, for staring out of the dust jacket was a superb photograph of Trocchi: the tousled hair; the thin, angular face with its strong chin and prominent nose; the broad, seemingly guileless smile. But it was the eyes that revealed—or at least suggested—

the monster: they smiled, too, but only to seduce, to charm, to cajole, and, yes, to con. It is the Trocchi I knew in Paris in the 1950s, then later in New York where he lived and wrote *Cain's Book*. It is the Trocchi who describes himself in that "novel":

> I also am tall. I was wearing my heavy white seaman's jersey with a high polo neck, and I sensed that the angularity of my face—big nose, high cheekbones, sunken eyes—was softened by the shadows and smoothed—the effect of the drug—out of its habitual nervousness.

I met Trocchi just after he had brought out the first issue of an English-language magazine published in Paris, intriguingly entitled *Merlin*. There were half a dozen writers and poets involved—English, American, Canadian, South African—and I became one of them. Ranging in age from our early to mid twenties, we were all, despite the disparity of our geographies and backgrounds, deadly serious about Literature and Life. Of course we were in Paris for reasons partly romantic, but we differed from the so-called Lost Generation in several respects: Paris may have been our mistress, but the political realities of the time were our master. This was the dawn of the Atomic Era, and the Cold War was upon us: the world was divided into camps no longer armed with simple guns but with the weapons of the apocalypse. Richard Nixon was in Washington, and so was Joe McCarthy, whose unofficial envoys, Cohn and Schine, came rampaging through Europe sowing fear and distrust. Stalin was paranoid, but not, it seemed to us, without some reason. And the first of those seemingly endless wars, Korea, was in full swing, bleeding America of more than its GIs' blood.

There was no way we could remain neutral, for neutrality was the death of the soul. In the debate between Camus and Sartre that rent the European literary establishment in those days, we clearly sided with the political scrapper over the detached philosopher, the *engagé* over the *non-engagé*. We were not just different from our Paris-based elders who had filled the cafés of Montparnasse in the twenties, we were the extreme opposite: pure literature in the sense that a Joyce or a Gertrude Stein understood it, experimentation as an end in itself, seemed to us impossible.

The first issues of *Merlin* could not have exceeded sixty-four pages, but each bore the weight of the early Cold War world on its meager shoulders.

In this context, Trocchi struck me, and I believe all of us, as the most talented and prepossessing writer on the scene, the one who, had a straw poll been taken, would have been voted most likely to become our generation's Joyce or Hemingway or—more likely—Orwell. Compared with Trocchi, who was only a year or two older than most of us, we were babes in the woods, fumbling toward knowledge or the hope of knowledge. He on the contrary was sure of himself, and his writing reflected it. He had already been married and divorced, was the father of two beautiful (albeit abandoned) daughters. He had already published stories and poems and was putting the finishing touches to his first novel, *Young Adam*, in which several British and American houses had expressed interest. That existentialist novel, as grim as the times in which it was written, was an exceptional first work, written from the same viewpoint and suffused with the same fervor that motivated *Merlin*: man is alone, and though he may not be responsible for what fate has meted out to him, that does not mean that responsibility can be sloughed off like some reptilian skin.

During those *Merlin* years I was as close to Trocchi as I have ever been to any friend or colleague. We talked endlessly about every subject, serious or frivolous; we sweated the publication of the magazine, always short of funds; we launched an ambitious and monetarily mad book publication venture. We worked together closely, and always in harmony.

Why then, rereading *Cain's Book* thirty-plus years after its original American publication, do I have such a feeling of pleasure on the one hand and anger on the other?

Explanation of the pleasure is easy. In 1960, Norman Mailer, never a pushover for compliments to competitors, wrote of *Cain's Book*: "It is true, it has art, it is brave. I would not be surprised if it is still talked about in twenty years." How does it stand up, not two but three decades later? How many books can withstand the erosion of time, the weight of their own shortcomings, the change of interests and sensibilities, the ever-evolving political realities? *Cain's Book* does stand up, amazingly well. The prose is taut and still fresh; the metaphors are striking and accurate. One can open the book to almost any page:

Fay's face was more reserved. Swinish? More like a pug than a pig. Her untidy dark hair tumbled into her big fur collar. A yellow female pigdog, her face in its warm nest beginning to stir with knowing.

But the inauthenticity was in the words, clinging to them like barnacles to a ship's hull, a growing impediment.

Tom Tear . . . was leaning backwards against the wall and his soft black eyelashes stirred like a clot of moving insects at his eyes. His face had the look of smoke and ashes, like a bombed city.

Jody loved cakes. She loved cakes and horse and all the varieties of soda pop. I knew what she meant. Some things surprised me at first, the way for example she stood for hours like a bird in the middle of the room with her head tucked in at her breast and her arms like drooping wings. At first this grated on me, for it meant the presence of an element unresolved in the absolute stability created by the heroin. She swayed as she stood, dangerous as Pisa.

Other qualities: Trocchi has dealt with the tough subject of drugs and the junkie life with rare truth and candor. There is no romanticism here—although several reviewers have likened *Cain's Book* to De Quincey and Baudelaire—the addict aware that he is "the loneliest man in the world." Honesty toward oneself is the linchpin of this clearly autobiographical work: Trocchi/Necchi isolated from the world; the outsider by choice but now, through drugs, by necessity; Cain, the violent and inviolable; the mole who burrows beneath the surface of the "normal" world, like Sade, the eternal *homme révolté*, yet as harsh and unrelenting about himself as he is about the bourgeois society he detests.

Only the proselytizing strikes me today as heavier and more obvious than I had remembered it, but thirty years ago I had argued to edit out some if not much of it, and lost. An editor's role is to suggest, not dictate, and the soapbox was very much an element in Trocchi's existence in 1960, as he railed against the world he had chosen and battled the authorities to keep out of jail. In fact, I suspect it was the battle itself that Trocchi relished, for it constantly resituated him in his self-proclaimed role of underground man, of bold warrior against misguided authority, a latter-day Sade who was convinced that the blind laws and callow mores of the day were not only hypocritical but directed specifically against him.

The parallel with Sade is more than superficial. Like the "divine Marquis," Trocchi used his "malady"—drugs—to forge a work of art. True, his meaningful opus is painfully thin compared to the massive legacy of Donatien-Alphonse, but in contrast to sexual obsession, drugs debilitate, render the user remote both in time and space, and are ultimately lethal, not only to himself but to those around him, as Trocchi's life all too sadly attests. Sade's sexual fantasies, coupled with his constant rage against society, goaded him to greater and greater eloquence and provocation. Trocchi's increasing immersion into the world of drugs—which he explained, using historical and literary precedents, as both willful and necessary to his artistic and personal fulfillment—withered his exceptional creative gifts. And they *were* exceptional: I remember vividly first reading the then incomplete manuscript of *Young Adam*, and marveling at both style and content, at the ease with which the sentences and paragraphs rolled from Trocchi's battered typewriter. The creator and self-critic were in perfect harmony, and the author's assurance contained not a whit of arrogance. That talent was also manifest in those days in Trocchi's writings and manifestos in *Merlin*, and even in the work-for-hire novels he produced with amazing speed for Maurice Girodias's burgeoning Olympia Press.

What a change, then, when ten years later, as the editor at Grove Press working on what was to become *Cain's Book*—the tentative title for which, by the way, was "Notes towards the Making of the Monster"—I witnessed the painful effort with which each page, each paragraph, each sentence was wrested onto the blank page. Since money was Trocchi's daily obsession, and he had spent twice over the advance the contract called for, we had reached an agreement—echoing the opening pages of a novel both Trocchi and I admired perhaps above all others, Samuel Beckett's *Molloy*—whereby Trocchi was given further small "advances" only as he turned in fresh pages. By then nothing came easy to Trocchi: he who in his ringing statements in the early issues of *Merlin* had set out to influence, if not to change the world (he was too canny to believe a literary magazine could actually change the world), now spent his waking hours hustling money in order to score—

in itself a full-time job—while at the same time dodging the evil forces of the law. Drugs not only set the user apart from society, but in Trocchi's view set him on the high moral ground where all is permitted and all excused. Whether one agrees with the premise—and I speak not only of drugs-as-truth but of any moral or immoral equivalent—the fact remains that *Cain's Book* documents a life, and a view, with rare power and insight.

James Campbell, a Scottish critic who confesses to the youthful and abiding influence of *Cain's Book* on his own life and view of the world, wrote recently in *London Magazine* that *Cain's Book* is not a "masterpiece" but a "mastercrime," a "book to give to minors, a book to corrupt young people." For there is no question that Trocchi set out if not to corrupt then certainly to shock, precisely as Sade had two centuries before him. His is an insidious message: play is more important than work; drugs are mind-expanding, ergo a positive force; laws are made and meant to be flouted; morals and mores are so much claptrap (this from a man who not only turned his new young American wife on to heroin but also reputedly put her out on the streets of Las Vegas as a hooker a scant six months after their marriage, a man who clearly practiced what he preached).

"I am outside your world," Trocchi wrote to a friend in the 1960s, not long after he had forsaken St.-Germain-des-Prés for Greenwich Village, "and am no longer governed by your laws." The problem was—and in his heart of hearts he knew this—in coming to America in the late

1950s Trocchi was consciously entering enemy territory, a climate far more hostile toward drugs than almost any other place on earth he might have chosen. However outside the law he was in his mind, the laws did exist and, as events proved, he could not avoid them. When he fled the country in 1961, wearing, it should be noted for the record, not one but two of George Plimpton's suits (and therein lies a whole other tale), it was with the threat of a death penalty hanging over his head, and his wife languishing in a stateside prison. Once I asked him whether this constant threat, this need forever to spend his day looking over his shoulder, was not utterly wearing, debilitating. "Not at all, Dick," he said convincingly, in his seductive, lilting Scottish accent, "on the contrary it's exhilarating to beat the bastards at their own dirty little game." Did he really believe that? Maybe in the short run; certainly not in the long.

When I wrote of Trocchi ten years or so ago, and expressed regret at what I felt, in the context of his great talent, was an unfulfilled promise, I received a scathing letter taking me to task for my arrogance. Who was I to pass judgment on him? How dare I express anger at what he did—or did not do—with his life? And of course he was right.

My anger, I realized, stemmed from my memory of that earlier Trocchi, my brother, of what he promised versus what he gave. I was angry at the junk that destroyed him—for destroy him it did. I was angry at the thought of the books he could have written and did not. To which Trocchi, again, would reply that it was not junk that destroyed him. Junk was but a tool, freely chosen and fully justified. It is a conversation we had had many times before, but, like the believer and the atheist, we had long since ceased to have any common ground for an unimpassioned discussion.

And yet, putting all this aside, and rereading *Cain's Book* once again after all these years, there is no doubt of its importance. With William Burroughs's *Naked Lunch*, it ranks as one of the best works to deal seriously and honestly with the subject of drugs. And as in the case of Burroughs's masterpiece, what some critics at the time of first publication attacked as its "formlessness" emerges as an integral and essential element of its enduring value. It is a book not to be taken lightly. It has, as James Campbell notes, "been banned, burned, prosecuted, refused by book distributors everywhere, condemned for its loving descriptions of heroin use and coarse sexual content. . . . *Cain's Book* is more than a novel: it is a way of life. The book is autobiography and fiction at once, the journal of a fiend, a stage-by-stage account of the junkie's odyssey in New York, an examination of the mind under the influence, a rude gesture in the face of sexual propriety, a commentary on literary processes and critical practices, a chart for the exploration of inner space."

"There is no more systematic nihilism than the Junkie in America," wrote the Scotsman Trocchi. In fact, as a description of that life, and that stance, *Cain's Book* is without peer in contemporary literature.

Richard Seaver
1992

. . . . *Their corruption is so dangerous, so active, that they have no other aim in printing their monstrous works than to extend beyond their own lives the sum total of their crimes; they can commit no more, but their accursed writings will lead others to do so, and this comforting thought which they carry with them to the tomb consoles them for the obligation death imposes on them of renouncing this life.*

—D.-A. F. de Sade

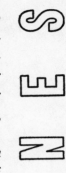

My scow is tied up in the canal at Flushing, N.Y., alongside the landing stage of the Mac Asphalt and Construction Corporation. It is now just after five in the afternoon. Today at this time it is still afternoon, and the sun, striking the cinderblocks of the main building of the works, has turned them pink. The motor cranes and the decks of the other scows tied up round about are deserted.

Half an hour ago I gave myself a fix.

I stood the needle and the eye-dropper in a glass of cold water and lay down on the bunk. I felt giddy almost at once. It's good shit, not like some of the stuff we've been getting lately. I had to be careful. Two of the workmen in wide blue dungarees and wearing baseball caps were still hanging about. From time to time they crossed my catwalk. They were inquisitive. They had heard the noise of the typewriter during the afternoon and that was suffi-

cient to arouse their curiosity. It's not usual for a scow
captain to carry a typewriter. They lingered for a while,
talking, just outside the cabin. Then, a few minutes before five, I heard them climb back on to the dock and
walk away.

Lying on the bunk, alert to the sudden silence that has
come over the canal, I hear the buzz of a fly and notice
it is worrying the dry corpse of another fly which is half-
gouged into the plank of the wall. I wonder about it and
then my attention wanders. A few minutes have passed.
I hear it buzz again and see that it is still at its work, whatever it is, settled on the rigid jutting legs of the corpse.
The legs grow out of the black spot like a minute sprout
of eyelashes. The live fly is busy. I wonder if it is blood
it wants, if flies like wolves or rats will eat off their own
kind.

—Cain at his orisons, Narcissus at his mirror.

The mind under heroin evades perception as it does
ordinarily; one is aware only of contents. But that whole
way of posing the question, of dividing the mind from
what it's aware of, is fruitless. Nor is it that the objects of
perception are intrusive in an electric way as they are
under mescalin or lysergic acid, nor that things strike one
with more intensity or in a more enchanted or detailed
way as I have sometimes experienced under marijuana; it
is that the perceiving turns inward, the eyelids droop, the
blood is aware of itself, a slow phosphorescence in all the

fabric of flesh and nerve and bone; it is that the organism has a sense of being intact and unbrittle, and, above all, *inviolable*. For the attitude born of this sense of inviolability some Americans have used the word "cool."

It is evening now, the temperature has fallen, objects are growing together in the dim light of the cabin. In a few moments I shall get up and light my kerosene lamps.

—What the hell am I doing here?
At certain moments I find myself looking on my whole life as leading up to the present moment, the present being all I have to affirm. It's somehow undignified to speak of the past or to think about the future. I don't seriously occupy myself with the question in the "here-and-now," lying on my bunk and, under the influence of heroin, inviolable. That is one of the virtues of the drug, that it empties such questions of all anguish, transports them to another region, a painless theoretical region, a play region, surprising, fertile, and unmoral. One is no longer grotesquely involved in the becoming. One simply is. I remember saying to Sebastian before he returned to Europe with his new wife that it was imperative to know what it was to be a vegetable, as well.

. . . the illusory sense of adequacy induced in a man by the drug. Illusory? Can a . . . "datum" be false? Inadequate? In relation to what? The facts? What facts? Marxian facts? Freudian facts? Mendelian facts? More and more I found it necessary to suspend such facts, to exist simply in abeyance, to give up (if you will), and come naked to apprehension.

It's not possible to come quite naked to apprehension and for the past year I have found it difficult to sustain even an approximate attitude without shit, horse, heroin. Details, impressionistic, lyrical. I became fascinated by the minute to minute sensations and when I reflected I did so repetitively and exhaustingly (often under marijuana) on the meaningless texture of the present moment, the cries of gulls, a floating spar, a shaft of sunlight, and it wasn't long before the sense of being alone overtook me and drained me of all hope of ever entering the city with its complicated relations, its plexus of outrageous purpose.

—The facts. Stick to the facts. A fine empirical principle, but below the level of language the facts slide away like a lava. Neither was there ever a simple act; in retrospect I couldn't isolate such a thing. Even while I lived in my act, at each phase, after the decidings, it unfolded spontaneously, and frighteningly, and dangerously, at times like a disease run riot, at times like the growing morning sunlight, and if I find it difficult to remember and express, and difficult to express and remember, if sometimes words leap up, sudden, unnatural, squint and jingling skeletons from the page, accusing me and amusing me with their obscene shakes and making the world mad, I suppose it is because they take a kind of ancestral revenge upon me who at each moment is ready to marshal them again for death or resurrection. No doubt I shall go on writing, stumbling across tundras of unmeaning, planting words like bloody flags in my wake. Loose ends, things unrelated, shifts, nightmare journeys, cities arrived at and left, meetings, desertions, betrayals, all manner of unions, adulteries, triumphs, defeats . . . these are the facts. It's a fact that in the America I found nothing was ever in abeyance. Things moved or they were subversive. I suppose it was to escape this without going away, to retreat into abeyance, that I soon came to be on a river scow. (Alternatives: prison, madhouse, morgue.)

I get up off the bunk and return to the table where I light an oil-lamp. When I have adjusted the wick I find myself fumbling again amongst the pile of notes, extracting a certain page. I hold it close to the lamp and read:

—Time on the scows. . . .

Day and night soon became for me merely light and dark, daylight or oil-lamp, and often the lamp became pale and transparent in the long dawns. It was the warmth of the sun that came on my cheek and on my hand through the window which made me get up and go outside and find the sun already far overhead and the skyscrapers of Manhattan suddenly and impressively and irrelevantly there in a haze of heat. And as for that irrelevance . . . I often wondered how far out a man could go without being obliterated. It's an oblique way to look at Manhattan, seeing it islanded there for days on end across the buffering water like a little mirage in which one isn't involved, for at times I knew it objectively and with anxiety as a nexus of hard fact, as my very condition. Sometimes it was like trumpets, that architecture.

I find myself squirting a thin stream of water from the eye-dropper through the number 26 needle into the air, cooking up another fix, prodding the hardened cotton in the bubbling spoon . . . just a small fix, I feel, would re-create the strewn ramparts of Jericho.

Tout ce qu'on fait dans la vie, même l'amour, on le fait dans le train express qui roule vers la mort. Fumer l'opium, c'est quitter le train en marche; c'est s'occuper d'autre chose que de la vie, de la mort.

—Cocteau

At 33rd Street is Pier 72. At the waterfront there are few buildings and they are low. The city is in the background. It has diners at its edge, boxcars abandoned and stored, rails amongst grass and gravel, vacant lots. The trucks of moving and storage companies are parked and shunted under the tunnels of an area of broad deserted shadows, useful for murder or rape. The wharves jut forward into the Hudson River like the stunted uneven teeth of a prehistoric jaw. The George Washington Bridge is in the north. After eight, when the diners close, the dockside streets are fairly deserted. In winter the lights under the elevated roadway shine as in a vast and dingy shed, dimly reflecting its own emptiness. An occasional car moves in from the dark side of the crosstown streets, turns into the feebly-lit dockyard area, travels ten or twenty blocks south, and then moves out, outwards again into the city. Walk three blocks east to

Ninth Avenue and the lights get brighter. A woman bawls her husband's affairs to a neighbour in the street from the window in which she leans thirty feet above your head as you walk along.

Pier 72 is the one immediately north of the new heliport which lies in the southern end of the basin formed by Piers 72 and 71. The remainder of the basin is used to moor the scows of a stone corporation with quarries at Haverstraw, Tomkin's Cove, and Clinton Point on the Hudson River. Piers 72 and 73 are close together. Nine scows at most are moored there. Looking in from the river you see the gabled ends of two huge and dilapidated barns perched on foundations of stones and heavy beams, with a narrow walk round three sides of each. The gable-end of Pier 73 is a landmark from the river because it is painted with red, white, and blue stripes representing American Lines. At the end of Pier 72 there is a small landing-stage set with bollards and cleats of cast iron. A little wooden box painted green is nailed to the gable end of the shed. It houses lists from the dispatcher's office of the crushed stone corporation, lists which pertain to the movements of the scows.

An hour ago I smoked some marijuana which came from Chile. It was particularly good. But for me it is an ambiguous drug. It can induce control or hysteria, and sometimes a terrifying and enervating succession of moods, new beginnings, generated spontaneously in the unwatched part of oneself . . . slow, quick, switchback, tumbling away from oneself in a sickening fashion, and then, suddenly, being in control. This can be exhausting.

Intense concentration on an external object suddenly shatters, and one has a fleeting, ambiguous glimpse of one's own pale face. The cause of what is to be shunned is the junction of the seer and the seen. The ordinary logic of association ceases to be operative. The problem, if one takes the trouble to pose it at all, is to find a new criterion of relevance. Understandably, at such times, the list in the box at the end of Pier 72, indicating as it does the hour at which a tug will arrive to take one's scow in tow, has a fatality about it. One had hoped to go into the Village on arrival at the pier but on reading the list one finds one's scow amongst those to be picked up immediately.

This particular night—it was in the middle of winter—I was not on the list. I went over it twice very carefully, running my finger down the column of scows, O'Brien, Macdougal, Campbell, O'Malley, Matteotti, Leonard, Marshall, Cook, Smith, Peterson: Red Star, on arrival; Coogan, Baxter, Haynes, Loveday: Colonial, with the tide. There were a few scowmen hanging around the end of the pier, mostly those who were going out at once.

I went back to the scow. In the cabin I stowed away some things that were lying about, my hashish pipe, a bottle of benzedrine, locked the cabin and climbed over four scows and on to the pier. I walked along the huge beam which provides the narrow footpath parallel to the shed as far as the dock. I walked slowly, using a flashlight to guide my feet. On my left the corrugated iron of the shed, on my right, about fourteen feet below me, the still dark water of the basin reflecting a few naked lights. Its surface was smeared with oil and dust. Finally I reached the dock and walked between some parked boxcars to the street under the elevated road. I cut diagonally across town and at 23rd Street on Eighth Avenue I took a taxi to Sheridan Square. I telephoned Moira from the drugstore that sells all the paperbacks. She told me to come over.

She was glad to see me. We hadn't seen one another for over two weeks. —Have you taken dope? Nope. —Our conversation was sometimes limited. She had smoked pot for some years but her attitude towards heroin was rigid. It made our relationship tense and hysterical. Sometimes I wondered why I bothered to go to see her, and that was the way it was with most of my friends who didn't use junk. "It's none of my business," Moira said. "I've got no sympathy for them."

It would make me very angry when she said that. I wanted to shake her. "*You* say that! Sometimes I think of all those ignorant cops, all those ignorant judges, all those ignorant bastard people committing bloody murder like they blow their noses! They think it so fucking easy they can stamp it out like syphokles, whatever it is, jewry, heroin-addiction, like some kind of streptococcus, and getting high an un-American rabies, Jesus, to a healthy paranoid like me who likes four walls and police-locks on all doors and a couple of good Frankensteins to draw off the mob with their flaming torches, it looks like anyone who depicts you, dear Saviour, with a beard will be dealt with cold turkey until they take him before a judge and then, because it can't stand, being bestial, scarcely human, the quivering, blubbering, vomiting mass is given half a grain of morphine ten minutes before he is arraigned so that they won't have to take him in on a stretcher and run the risk of having some irresponsible goon send for a doctor!"

"It's none of my business!" Moira screamed.

"Whose business is it? What are you going to do? Leave it to the experts? Tomorrow, the Age of the Doctors! They're already challenging the tax men and the F.B.I. for a profitable monopoly. Let's put it on prescription, eh? confine it to the laboratories for more tests. They're always talking about a lack of scientific evidence, about its being unsafe to make it public! They're scared the public will find out it ain't that fucking horse after all!"

"*They're* scared! Who's *they?*"

"You! Dammit to hell, Moira! You!"

"I don't want to discuss it! I won't argue with you!"

At that moment the telephone rang. She was grateful for the distraction. But it was Tom Tear. As welcome as a newborn Mongolian idiot. He had heard I was in town and wanted to know if I wanted to score. She held her hand over the mouthpiece of the receiver and her face became angry as she became aware of my hesitation. She spoke coldly into the telephone: "He's here now. You'd better speak to him yourself." As she handed me the telephone she said she didn't want him telephoning me there. She avoided my disbelieving eyes and her face became set and hard. I could see only the back of her head now, the long blonde hair in a smooth bell. —I remember the first time I smelled it; her cheek was cold; it was the middle of winter and in Glasgow there was snow in the streets. By the time I turned my attention to the telephone I knew I

would score, that it was only a question of arranging the
time and the place. The thought of an evening with her
in her present mood was stifling. Tom's voice, because he
had been sensitive to the tone of Moira's, was apologetic,
almost wheedling. "Don't be so fucking sorry," I said to
him, watching her overhear. "Where'll I meet you?" A
place at Sheridan Square in half an hour's time. I put down
the telephone. Moira was pouring coffee.

I had to say something. I said: "Look, Moira, I know
what I'm doing."

"I don't want to talk about it," she said dully.

And we didn't. I wanted to explain and not to explain.
At the same time I considered her attitude impertinent.
I drank my coffee and left.

Fay was with Tom. Tom made the run alone and Fay
and I walked over together to his place from Sheridan
Square. We walked quickly so as to get there by the time
he returned with the heroin.

"It's going to be good, baby," Fay said.

The room has a low sloping ceiling with two small windows on one side and a fireplace with a raised brick hearth
in an opposite corner, at the far end of the adjacent side.
Sometimes Tom Tear burned a few sticks in the grate and
we sat with our knees at the level of the fire which cast
shadows on the dirty ceiling and walls and on the bricks
of the fireplace, the three of us on a small, backless couch
spread over with a fawn blanket, looking into the fire, Fay

in the centre, still wearing her moth-eaten fur coat, her arms folded, her head sunk on her chest, her slightly bulbous, yellowish eyes closed. We sat there after we had fixed and watched wood burn. The white boxwood burned quickly. Tom Tear leaned forward and added a few sticks to the blaze. He is a tall man in his late twenties, lean, with a beautiful, pale, lean face expressionless often as porcelain, the nose long, the eyes half-closed and heavily lidded under the drug.

I also am tall. I was wearing my heavy white seaman's jersey with a high polo neck, and I sensed that the angularity of my face—big nose, high cheekbones, sunken eyes —was softened by the shadows and smoothed—the effect of the drug—out of its habitual nervousness. My eyes were closed. My elbows rested on my thighs and my hands were clasped in front of me. Tom Tear is a negro who sometimes speaks dreamily of the West Indies.

At that moment I felt impelled to speak and I said: "My father had false teeth."

I was aware that I flashed a quick, intimate glance first at Tom, across Fay's line of vision, and then, turning my head slightly, I caught the glint of appraisal in her pale protruding eyes.

"Yes," I said, and my face grew radiant, encouraging them to listen, "he had yellow dentures."

Tom's teeth—they are long and yellowish and give his mouth a look of bone—were clenched in a tight smile, the pale lips falling away, exposing them. It was almost a mask of ecstasy, *part of the game*, I might have said in some contexts, in some rooms.

Fay's face was more reserved. Swinish? More like a pug than a pig. Her untidy dark hair tumbled into her big fur collar. A yellow female pigdog, her face in its warm nest beginning to stir with knowing.

"He was outside in the hall, spying on the lodgers," I said. "My father was a born quisling, and he had false teeth."

Tom Tear's face was patient and serene. The flicker of the fire stirred in the sparse black stubble on his lower face, making the hairs glint.

I went on for the friendly silence: "While he was in the hall his false teeth were squatting like an octopus in a glass of water on the kitchen dresser. The plates were a dark orange brick colour and the teeth were like discoloured piano keys. They seemed to breathe at the bottom of the glass. The water was cloudy and tiny bubbles clung to the teeth. That was the kitchen where we lived, and they sat there like a breathing eye, watching us."

Fay's bluish lips had fallen apart in a smile. She made a grunt of understanding through her decayed teeth. Fay is forty-two. She has lived all her life in this city.

Tom Tear leaned forward and threw more wood on the fire. Wood is plentiful. We gather it, when we can be bothered, on the streets.

"He went on tiptoe about the hall for nine years," I said, "in tennis shoes and without his teeth. The hall was No-man's Land."

Tom Tear nodded as he leaned back again away from the fire. His right cheek, which was all I saw from where I sat, was impassive, long and smooth.

"If someone came to the front door he came flying back into the kitchen for his teeth. He came in puffing and blowing with his hand on his paunch. He wore a collarless shirt with a stud in it and he went round in his shirt sleeves and this old grey, sleeveless pullover." I paused. A white stick darkened and burst into flame. "When he grew older he became less frantic about the teeth," I said, smiling. "He slipped them into his mouth furtively in front of the visitor as though he suddenly remembered and didn't want to give offence. Perhaps he no longer needed defences."

"He'd given up by that time," Fay said. She looked straight into the fire.

We were all silent for a moment. I felt I had to go on. I said: "I'll tell you a story. . . ."

The others smiled. Fay touched the back of my hand with her fingertips. I remember noticing she had prominent eye-teeth.

"It's not really a story," I said. "It's something I read somewhere, about a river bushman. This man wanted to track down some bushmen and he went to a place called Serongo in the swamps. One day he caught sight of a bushman paddling alone in a boat and he asked his head bearer if he would speak to him and get him to lead them to his tribe. The bearer told him he had known the bushman for thirty years, that he lived alone on a termite mound in the middle of the swamps, and he was deaf and dumb as well."

The others looked at me. I moved my clasped hands forward and stared at the thumbs. They were dirty at the knuckles and at the nails.

We were all silent.

"It's necessary to give up first," I began tentatively, "but it should be a beginning. . . ." I sensed an ambiguity, something not quite authentic, and stopped speaking.

"Go on," Tom said after a moment.

But the inauthenticity was in the words, clinging to them like barnacles to a ship's hull, a growing impediment. I shook my head, closed my eyes.

Again we were all silent. The smoke from the burning wood wound its way towards the chimney, some of it spilling outwards into the room where it clung to the low ceiling.

"Does anyone want to go out?" Fay said.

When neither of us answered she made the motion of snuggling inside her warm fur coat. "It's cold outside, too cold," she said.

I was sitting hunched forward with my eyes closed, my chin deep in the high woollen collar. The phrase "*ex nihil nihil fit*" had just come to me. It seemed to me that nothing would be beginning, ever.

Tom Tear, who a moment before had moved to a stool at the side of the fireplace, was leaning backwards against the wall and his soft black eyelashes stirred like a clot of moving insects at his eyes. His face had the look of smoke and ashes, like a bombed city. It was at rest, outwardly.

There is a bed in the room, a low double bed on which three dirty grey army blankets are stretched. On the wall between the two square windows—they are uncurtained and at night the four panes of glass in each are black and glossy—is a faded engraving, unframed. It curls away from the wall at one corner where the scotch tape has come away. There are two similar engravings on two other walls, both of them warped and one of them with a tear at the corner. On the fourth wall there is an unskilful pencil sketch of some trees and a water colour of a woman's face, vague and pink, and painted on flimsy paper. This is the work of Tom Tear's girlfriend. A self-portrait. He talks of her now and again, always vaguely. She is kicking her habit in some clinic out of town. The last piece of furniture apart from the backless couch and the stool on which Tom Tear sat is a draughtsman's table which tilts on a ratchet to any required angle. This is the table on which Tom Tear will work if ever he becomes an architect. At that moment the table was horizontal and there was a clock on it, and an electric lamp which didn't work, and a burning candle, and a radio with a plastic cabinet in which another clock was inlaid. Both clocks said twenty-five past nine. That was all there was on the table, apart from the spike, and the glass of water, and the spoon.

We had fixed over an hour ago. We had used all the heroin.

Each of us was conscious of the well-being of the others. The blaze of wood in the fireplace made our cheeks glow. Our faces were smooth, and serene.

"I can't do with it and I can't do without it," Fay had said earlier as she prodded the back of her left hand—the flesh was thin there and waxy—in search of a possible vein. At the third attempt she found a vein and the blood rose up through the needle into the eye-dropper and appeared as a dark red tongue in the colourless solution. "Hit," she said softly, with a slow smile. When she put the eye-dropper with the needle attached back into the glass of water and dabbed the back of her bluish hand with tissue paper there was no longer any fear in her eyes, only certainty, and in their yellowish depths ecstasy. I knew at that moment she was impregnable. I laughed softly at her and touched the slack flesh of her cheek lightly with my fingers. At that moment I was happy for her and I knew that she, when she watched me fix a moment later, would be happy for me.

Each of us was conscious of the well-being of the others. The sense of well-being in each of us was reinforced by that consciousness.

I said suddenly that the wheel hadn't been invented yet.

"What's a wheel?" Tom Tear said.

We were sitting, three absent faces towards the fire, a crude fire, and gloom beyond our shoulders. Fay's moth-eaten fur coat was gathered under her chin like an old animal skin. "Outside," Fay said, her protruding yellow eyes glinting dully in the firelight, "there is the jungle." She laughed huskily and laid her friendly blue hand on my knee.

Tom's face, tilted towards the ceiling, was idyllic, in-violable.

"And it's raining outside," she said softly.

A moment later, she said: "You said your father was a spy, Joe. You mean he was inquisitive?"

I said: "The job he had before he became unemployable was a spy's job. He was a musician to begin with but he became a spy. His job was to snoop round clubs and concert halls to see that no one infringed copyrights. He was the fuzz, the executioner, the Man. He was always closing curtains. . . ." I leaned across and whispered loudly in Fay's ear, "Don't you know that people can see in?"

I said: "In the end he identified himself so completely with Authority that he became unemployable, he took too much upon himself, he felt himself free to make executive decisions, even if he was only the doorman. When he was summoned during the war for selling confectionery at black market rates without coupons—he sold it by the quarter pound to anyone who expressed conservative sentiments—he ranted against Socialism and red tape. When he was arrested for soliciting on the street he pleaded with tears in his eyes that he was only trying to control a queue."

Fay was poking at the fire with a stick, smiling like a yellow idol.

"I'll go and break some more wood," I said. I got up and moved over to the door. As I opened it Tom's dog bounded in. "That damn dog again," I heard Fay say as I crossed the large, low studio, now brimming over with lumber and other materials, into which the door led. I selected a flimsy box and began breaking it into pieces.

When I returned to the room with my arms full of broken sticks, the terrier, an old bone in its mouth, was growling. That dog has a mad eye. I looked down at the shaggy brown head, at the shining wet fangs, at the mad eyeball, and I said quietly: "What a fucking animal!"

"Get out!" Tom Tear yelled at the dog. "Get out of here you ill-mannered bitch!" He got up, grabbed the dog by the collar, and ran it rigid-legged into the next room.

I put the sticks down near the fireplace and added a few to the flames.

"He should get rid of it," Fay said before Tom returned.

"He's mad," I said. "You know a few nights ago in the street another dog tried to mount her. Tom went stark raving mad."

"I don't want her knocked up by any lousy mongrel!" Fay mimicked.

"That dog is me," Tom said once. And it is. It is vicious and untrustworthy and it bites his friends. "She was badly treated by her first owner!" She attacked anyone who tried to feed her. Like Tom, she never had a chance. Anger, innocence; the voice of the oppressed.

"Jesus," Fay said, "all that sentimental crap makes me sick. I don't know why he doesn't get rid of it!"

He came back, closing the door behind him. The dog whimpered on the far side of it. Tom sat down again and for a while none of us spoke.

"Seen Jody lately?" Fay asked me.

"No. Have you?"

Fay shook her head. "Tom saw her yesterday," she said. I looked over at Tom.

"At Sheridan Square," he said. "She wanted to turn on but she didn't have any bread."

"How was she?" I said mechanically. The question came from a theoretical part of me, and yet I was involved in it, and I was more interested than either of the others knew. I suppose I loved Jody. At least I had often found myself acting as though I did. But it wouldn't bear analysis and I enjoyed it as a sensation, intense, fragile, relative, a state of being, a hint of possibility. If Jody had been in the room at that moment, lying on the bed, and if she had said: "Come and lie down beside me, Joe," I would have gone and lain down beside her.

"O.K.," Tom said. "She looked O.K."

But I had no impulse to go out and look for her. If I had known then she was sitting in Jim Moore's Diner I wouldn't have walked over to Sheridan Square to pick her up.

"You mean she was sweating her ass off for a fix but she was looking all the same fine, Tom?"

"Yeah!" Fay said.

"She doesn't sweat much," Tom said. "She's not hooked."

Listening to the tone of his voice I wondered why he didn't like Jody. I have asked him more than once but he's always evasive in his replies. Of course I can understand anyone's not liking Jody.

"She's no chippie, man!" Fay said to Tom, fixing her bilious yellow eyes on him. They glinted like yellow ivory in the firelight.

Tear said he didn't say she was but that she didn't use enough to have a real habit.

"A 'real' habit," Fay said ironically. "She takes all she can get, man."

"She could hustle, she could boost more," Tear said.

"Sure, she could make a profession of it." I said.

"That's the trouble in this damn country," Fay said. "You take shit and it becomes your profession."

. . . Feed my habit, I was thinking. That's what Moira said to me: "Jody! She just uses you! She lies in her little nest and waits for you to come and feed her. She's like a bird, a fat, greedy little bird!" The thought only amused me. It wasn't that it hadn't occurred to me. Jody would burn me mercilessly. I amused myself by telling Moira that I loved Jody. "And she loves you, I suppose! You're a fool, Joe! She loves horse. My God, it makes me mad! And you come to me for money to buy shit for her! She doesn't even let you screw her!" "Yes, that's too much," I said quickly, "but it doesn't matter, Moira, not in the way you think, and not as much as you think it does." I remember Jody saying: "When we do make love, Joe, it'll be the end!" The end-love, she meant, the ultimate. —Like an overdose, Jody?

"When you're not straight," Fay said, "you're looking for it or looking for money to get it with."

"It simplifies things," I said with a smile. "Are you ready to simplify things and become a professional, Tom?"

Fay laughed huskily.

"I'm gonna kick tomorrow," Tear said woodenly, leaning his long hands towards the fire.

We both looked at him.

"I mean it, fuck it all," he said in a slow, laconic voice. "I've been on this kick long enough. It's no fucking good. I spend most of my time in the subway. Backwards and forwards. To cop."

"Yeah," Fay said. Her lip drooped in a smile as she poked the fire again. "It's a big drag."

Of course I knew I was playing with them as I always played. And they were playing with me and with each other. I wondered whether it wasn't always like that. In all the living how could you expect other people to act except "as if?" At this point I was involved once again in the feeling of thinking something not quite authentic and I allowed the heroin to come back and take me entirely, and then only the room existed, like a cave, like "Castle Keep," and if other people existed it didn't matter, it didn't matter at all. The jungle could encroach no farther than the tips of my senses. No matter what went before, from the moment of the fix. And I thought again of Jody, and of how plump she is from eating too many cakes, of the soft wad of her belly, of our thighs without urgency interlaced, of her ugly bitten hands, of the mark on the back of her left hand, high, between forefinger and thumb . . . it looks like a small purple cyst . . . into which she drives the needle each time she fixes. "That's your cunt, Jody," I said once, and I remember how she looked at me, softly and speculatively, drawing out the needle and watching the bead of blood form on the back of her hand, how she put the hand then to my mouth.

"Even without dollies," Tom Tear said, "I could kick it in three days."

"Sure, three days is plenty," Fay said elliptically. She clasped her hands at her knees and leaned forward towards the fire to lay her chin on them.

"I wouldn't need dollies," Tear said, leaning backwards again and closing his eyes.

"What would you do all day if you didn't have to look for a fix?" I said to him.

"You write," Fay said, glancing sideways and upwards at me. "*Cain* is great."

"Yeah, not necessarily for anyone else. It's all I've got except Now . . . you know?"

"Sure," Fay said. "It's evidence."

"Yeah, Kilroy was here."

"I want to read it," Tom said. (He never will. He's afraid of evidence. He acts all the time with a kind of eager anti-intelligence, like his own mad dog, in the teeth of evidence.)

"Any time," I said. "I wrote it for us. It's a textbook for dope fiends and other moles."

Fay laughed huskily.

"It's great," she said. "What was it about the gallows, Joe?"

I smiled with pleasure at being able to quote myself.

"*If a gallows is clean, what more can a criminal expect?*"

I showed Jody *Cain's Book*. Something prevented her from having any response whatsoever. She said she couldn't understand it. She looked blank and shook her head.

"Nothing?" I said incredulously.

Fay understood at once. Tom didn't. He rubbed his woolly head. His dog has the same woolly hair, only it's chestnut. But Fay understood. "That's it," she said. "You gotta keep at it. You gotta do something. If you don't do anything it's a big drag. If I could only get a place to work!"

"Go to Mexico or back to Paris," I said. "You'd have to get out of this whole context. Here in New York you can only do as you're doing. Better make it Paris. In Mexico it costs more than it does here, just the atmosphere's better."

"You can say that again," Fay said. She added irrelevantly: "It's no good without a pad where I can work."

There's always something irrelevant. I had heard it all before. But I hesitate to deny all validity to this kind of talk. And when someone who hasn't used junk speaks easily of junkies I am full of contempt. It isn't simple, any kind of judgment here, and the judgments of the uninitiated tend to be stupid, hysterical. Anger and innocence . . . those virgin sisters again. No, when one presses the bulb of the eye-dropper and watches the pale, blood-streaked liquid disappear through the nozzle and into the needle and the vein it is not, not only, a question of feeling good. It's not only a question of kicks. The ritual itself, the powder in the spoon, the little ball of cotton, the matches applied, the bubbling liquid drawn up through the cotton filter into the eye-dropper, the tie round the arm to make a vein stand out, the fix often slow because a man will stand there with the needle in the vein and allow the level in the eye-dropper to waver up and down, up and down, until there is more blood than heroin in the dropper—all this is not for nothing; it is born of a respect for the whole chemistry of alienation. When a man fixes he is turned on almost instantaneously . . . you can speak of a flash, a

tinily murmured orgasm in the bloodstream, in the central
nervous system. At once, and regardless of preconditions,
a man enters "Castle Keep." In "Castle Keep," and even
in the face of the enemy, a man can accept. . . . I can
see Fay in her fur coat walking in the city at night close
to walls. At every corner a threat; the Man and his finks
are everywhere. She moves like a beast full of apprehension and for the Man and the values he seeks to impose on
her she has the beast's unbounded contempt.

A few hundred years ago Fay would have been burned
as a witch and she would have hurled curses and insults at
her destroyers from the stake, the unkempt black hair
alive with shock, her gleaming yellow eyes mad, and her
whole face contorted and hideous with hate to override
her pain. Who knows how she may die today? Limits have
been closing in; you can hang for dealings with a minor,
or rather, you can be electrocuted. Perhaps that is how Fay
will die, strapped to a very old-fashioned looking chair
. . . it is a curious fact that the death-chair has such a
quaint old-fashioned look! . . . whinnying hate through
purple nostrils, her outraged torso exuding blue smoke. But
for the moment she is a forlorn figure slipping quickly
through dark streets, desperate for a private place, for a
burrow, for "Castle Keep." There in that low-ceilinged
room, I had often said to Fay and to Tom that there was
no way out but that the acceptance of this could itself be
a beginning. I talked of plague, of earthquake, as being no
longer contemporary, of the death of tragedy which made
the diarist more than ever necessary. I exhorted them to

accept, to endure, to record. As a last act of blasphemy I exhorted them to be ready to pee on the flames.

"Jesus," Fay said suddenly, "I could use another fix."

"It's infectious," I said.

"I can get bread tomorrow," Fay said. "Couldn't you borrow a dime from Moira, Joe? I could give you it tomorrow. I'm going uptown tomorrow."

"Not a chance. We're hardly on speaking terms."

"Where's your boat?" Tom said.

"Pier 72."

"If we could only borrow a dime," Fay said. "There must be someone."

"You hit him last night," Tom said. "Why don't you go out and turn a trick?"

"D'you think I wouldn't?"

Past forty, and with her blue look, Fay finds it difficult to interest a John . . . Dracula's idea of a good lay. Since she got back from Lexington (the second time) her habit has re-entrenched itself. From day to day I watched her retreat being cut off, and I knew that if I said to her: "Fay, you're cutting off your retreat," she would say she knew and that she was going to kick tomorrow, a perfectly valid answer if you are a junkie. Fay could say she was going to kick tomorrow without compromising herself in any way. Fixed, she was in the citadel, and such justifications as came to mind were transparent, of no weight, not part

of her affective living. She was inviolate. Talking to Fay
you have the impression you are speaking to the secretary
of her personal secretary. There is no question of her
being capped. It's a religion for her and she is the only
member of the church. That's often said about Fay. It
becomes more and more difficult to get through to her.
It's not that she doesn't reply. It's simply you have the
impression you are in touch with an answering service,
that Fay herself is not speaking to you, that she will certainly not feel committed to anything that's agreed upon
between you and whoever it is that replies.

"Yes, baby," Fay says. Which means no, or perhaps,
or even yes. There's no way of telling. There is no more
systematic nihilism than that of the junkie in America.

I often felt during those months like a frantic fisherman
struggling grotesquely to hold on to the only fish I could
ever hope to catch. I couldn't say whether Fay felt she
had lost her fish. I supposed she didn't. Her movements
were those of a yellow ferret. There was always a lithe
quality in her caution. When she strikes she strikes quickly,
with bared teeth; she will burn anyone when she is desperate. She is known everywhere in the Village, but she
returns to her lair again and again unharmed. Whatever
lair. She has none of her own. Under heroin one adapts
oneself naturally to a new habitat. It is possible to live in
a doorway, on someone's couch, or bed, or floor, always
moving, and turning up from time to time at known places.
Fay, owning nothing but the clothes on her back and
ridden by her terrible craving, is more than anyone the
grey ghost of the district; she can always cop, and she has

burned everyone. She invokes horror, disgust, indignation, a nameless fear. She is the soul's scavenger, the unexpected guest, a kind of underworld Florence Nightingale always abroad with her spike and her little bag of heroin. She is beyond truth and falsity. When I think of her I think of her soft yellow pugface and her violet hands.

"It's no good," I said, "there's no one. No point in beating our brains."

"If I could just get a taste," Fay said.

"What are you going to do, Joe?" Tom said.

"Back to the scow. I may go out early in the morning, any time after eight."

"I'll walk you as far as Sheridan Square," Tom said. "I think I'll hang around there a while. I might run into something."

"What about you, Fay?"

"No. I'll stay here. Look, Tom, if you cop anything, bring it back, will you? I'm going uptown tomorrow, boost a good coat."

"Don't get caught," I said. "Why don't you take some of your sculptures up to that guy who's interested?"

"I would but I need something to wear. I can't go like this. An' I've got to have a fix before I go."

"Sure. O.K. Look after yourself. I'll see you."

"See you, Joe. Look, try to get back quick, will you, Tom?"

"Christ, I don't know if I'll get anything!"

"O.K., but hurry. . . ."

*When I was three I went to bed at
night with a stuffed white bird. It had
soft feathers and I held it close to my
face. But it was a dead bird and sometimes I looked at it hard and for a long
time. Sometimes I ran my thumbnail
along the split in the rigid beak. Sometimes I sucked the blue beads which
had been sewn in place of the eyes.
When the beak was prised open and
wouldn't close again I disliked the bird
and sought justifications. It was indeed
a bad bird.*

The past is to be treated with
respect, but from time to time it should be affronted, raped.
It should never be allowed to petrify. A man will find out
who he is. Cain, Abel. And then he will make the image
of himself coherent in itself, but only in so far as it is prudent will he allow it to be contradictory to the external
world. A man is contradicted by the external world when,
for example, he is hanged.

These thoughts come to mind . . . such is my drugged
state, the only witness myself, only the metamorphic
Count offering you eternal death, who has committed
suicide in an hundred obscene ways, an exercise in spiritual masturbation, a game well played when you are
alone . . . and I write them down as I try to feel my way
into where I left off.

I always find it difficult to get back to the narrative.
It is as though I might have chosen any of a thousand nar-

ratives. And, as for the one I chose, it has changed since yesterday. I have eaten, drunk, made love, turned on—hashish and heroin—since then. I think of the judge who had a bad breakfast and hanged the lout.

Cain's Book. When all is said and done, "my readers" don't exist, only numberless strange individuals, each grinding me in his own mill, for whose purpose I can't be responsible. No book was ever responsible. (Sophocles didn't fuck anyone's mother.) The feeling that this attitude requires defence in the modern world obsesses me.

God knows there are enough natural limits to human knowledge without our suffering willingly those that are enforced upon us by an ignorantly rationalized fear of experience. When I find myself walled in by the solid slabs of other men's fear I have a ferocious impulse to scream from the rooftops. —Yah bleedin mothahfuckahs! So help me Ah'll pee on you!— Prudence restrains me. But as the past must sometimes be affronted so also must prudence sometimes be overruled. *Caveat.*

I say it is impertinent, insolent, and presumptuous of any person or group of persons to impose their unexamined moral prohibitions upon me, that it is dangerous both to me and, although they are unaware of it, to the imposers, that in every instance in which such a prohibition becomes crystallized in law an alarming precedent is created. History is studded with examples, the sweet leper stifled by the moral prejudice of his age. Vigilance. Dispute legal precedent.

In my study of drugs (I don't pretend for a moment that my sole interest in drugs is to study their effects. . . To be familiar with this experience, to be able to attain, by whatever means, the serenity of a vantage point "beyond" death, to have such a critical technique at one's disposal— let me say simply that on my ability to attain that vantage point my own sanity has from time to time depended)—in my study of drugs I have been forced to run grave risks, and I have been stymied constantly by the barbarous laws under which their usage is controlled. These crude laws and the social hysteria of which they are a symptom have from day to day placed me at the edge of the gallow's leap. *I demand that these laws be changed.*

The hysterical gymnastics of governments confronting the problem of the atomic bomb is duplicated exactly in their confrontation of heroin. Heroin, a highly valuable drug, as democratic statistics testify, comes in for all the shit-slinging. Perhaps that is why junkies, many of whom possess the humour of detachment, sometimes call it "shit."

We cannot afford to leave the potential power of drugs in the hands of a few governmental "experts," whatever they call themselves. Critical knowledge we must vigilantly keep in the public domain. A cursory glance at history should caution us thus. I would recommend on grounds of public safety that heroin (and all other known drugs) be placed with lucid literature pertaining to its use and abuse on the counters of all chemists (to think that a man should be allowed a gun and not a drug!) and sold openly to anyone over twenty-one. This is the *only* safe method of controlling the use of drugs. At the moment we are encouraging ignorance, legislating to keep crime in existence, and preparing the way for one of the most heinous usurpations of power of all times . . . all over the world. . .

Such might have been my thoughts as I walked away from Sheridan Square where I left Tom Tear. He went into Jim Moore's. Sometimes he sat there for hours, usually in the middle of the night from about twelve till three or four; the countermen liked him and they were generous when he ordered anything. The diner, because it was open all night, was a useful meeting place. The coffee counter is composed of two U's linked by a very short counter which supports the cash register. Its top is of green plastic. The stools are red and chrome. There is a jukebox, a cigarette machine, glass everywhere, and windows . . . that's the advantage of the place, the huge uncurtained windows which look out on to the centre of the square. You can only sit there so long without being seen by your little junkie friends who can see you waiting. It's like being in a goldfish bowl in a display window of a pet shop. (In New York people look in at you through the glass windows of snack bars; Paris cafés spill out on to the street where those who are walking by are open to inspection.) It has also, from another point of view, its disadvantage. If our friends can look in, so can the police, and many of the anonymous men who sit at the counter or who lounge about outside in the small hours could conceivably fink. So it is dangerous to be seen there too often, especially if

you are high. Most of us returned there eventually because
we were often hung up for shit.

He had asked me to go and have a coffee with him but
I knew that once I was inside I would find it difficult to
leave. And of all the hours I spent, the hours of vigil I
spent in that diner, waiting, were probably the worst.

I walked up Seventh Avenue and turned west on 23rd
Street and made directly for the river. The bars were still
open so the streets weren't deserted. On 23rd a police car
trailed me for a few seconds and then glided past. Without
turning my head I caught a glimpse of the man beside the
driver, his head turned my way. I wasn't carrying anything that night.

I kept walking past Eighth, Ninth, and I walked up
Ninth and turned left a few blocks later. I was walking
slowly. Suddenly I was opposite an alley and in the alley
about twenty yards away was the dark figure of a man
standing close to a wall. He was alone under a small light
near a garage door and he was exposing himself to a brick
wall.

In terms of literal truth my curiosity was pointless. A
man goes to a lane to urinate, an everyday happening
which concerns only himself and those who are paid to
prevent public nuisance. It concerned me only because I
was there and doing nothing in particular as was quite
ordinary for me, like a piece of sensitive photographic
paper, waiting passively to feel the shock of impression.
And then I was quivering like a leaf, more precisely like
a mute hunk of appetitional plasm, a kind of sponge in

which the business of being excited was going on, run through by a series of external stimuli; the lane, the man, the pale light, the flash of silver—at the ecstatic edge of something to be known.

The flash of silver comes from earlier; it was a long time ago in my own country and I saw a man come out of an alley. He had large hands. The thought of his white front with its triangle of coarse short hair came to me. I thought of the mane of a wolf, of the white Huns, perhaps because he stooped. Or perhaps because my own ears were pricked back and alert. In his other hand was the glint of something silver. As he walked past me he put his hands in his pockets. I looked after him. I realised I hadn't seen his face. Before I reached the corner he had turned into an adjacent street. I reached the intersection and he was entering a public house. I didn't see him in the bar nor in any of the side rooms. The bar was crowded with workmen, the same caps, the same white scarves, the same boots. He was not in the men's toilet.

Sitting there—an afterthought—I noticed that someone had cut a woman's torso deep in the wood of the door. As big as a fat sardine. There was no toilet paper. I used a folded sheet of the *Evening News*, part of which I tore carefully from the other part which was wet. It was water, and dust had collected. It had been jammed beneath the pipe under the cistern. The ink had run. I felt a necessity to read inside the wet pages. When I peeled them apart

I found nothing of interest. A well-known stage actor was to be married. The paper was more than six weeks old. I remembered reading a few days before that he had since died. I couldn't remember whether he left a widow.

I drank one small whiskey at the bar and left. The original impulse to find him had left me. The street was deserted, and the lane. On my way home I wondered why I had followed him. I wasn't after facts, information. I didn't delude myself from the moment I became aware of his shadow, although in self-defence I may have pretended to wonder, to seek safety in the problematic. I can see now I must have known even then it was an *act* of curiosity. Even now I'm the victim of my own behaviour: each remembered fact of the congeries of facts out of which in my more or less continuous way I construct this document is an *act of remembrance*, a selected fiction, and I am the agent also of what is unremembered, rejected; thus I must pause, overlook, focus on my effective posture. My curiosity was a making of significance. I experienced a sly female lust to be impregnated by, beyond words and in a mystical way to confound myself with, not the man necessarily, though that was part of the possibility, but the secrecy of his gesture.

He wore the clothes of a workman, a cap, a shapeless jacket, and trousers baggy at the knees. He might have been a dustman, or a coalman, or unemployed. The hissing gas lamp cast his shadow diagonally across the lane and like a finger into the tunnel. As I came abreast of it I glanced through into the lane and when I saw him I caught my breath. The valve slid open. The faint lust at my belly made me conscious of the cold of the rest of my body. I felt the cool night wind on my face as I sensed my hesitation. It was the way he stood, swaying slightly, and half-hidden, and it was then that I thought of his crotch, and of the stench of goats in the clear night air of the Tartar steppes, of the hairs of his belly, and of the stream of yellow urine from his blunt prick running in a broad, steaming sheet down the stone wall, its precision geometrical, melting the snow near the toes of his big boots. If I had had the nerve I might have approached him then and there instead of following him to the bar, but there was no kinetic quality in my hesitation. It lay on me like an impotence, cloying, turning my feet to lead. It was my cowardice which shattered me. The other knowledge, of the desire, came as no shock. Still, and with a sense of bathos, I found myself moving in pursuit of him when he lurched backwards into full view and passed me at the end of the tunnel where I stood. Did I invent the glint of silver? Endow him with a non-existent razor. The honing of the blade. When I couldn't find him in the bar, and after I had applied my skill to the torso on the wooden door, I returned to the lane and walked through the tunnel towards light. The singing gas lamp evoked memories of sensation, but faintly, and there was no element of anticipation. In the lane I looked over the wall at the windows of the dark tenements above. A pale light showed here and there from behind curtains. Above the level of the roofs the sky was darkening indigo and shifty with thin cloud. I thought: on such a night as this werewolves are abroad and the ambulances of death run riot in the streets. I kicked at the

snow on the cobbles. My feet were cold. I walked home
with a sense of failure, too familiar even then to shrug off
easily. And then, when I entered the flat there was Moira
wearing her drop ear-rings, waiting, hoping, at the portal
of her day's thoughts, and I walked past her surlily, with
no greeting.

Moira was sitting opposite me. This was before our di-
vorce and before either of us came to America. I had put
the incident of the man in the lane out of my mind. It was
nearly ten o'clock. Two hours until the New Year. One
day followed another. Relief at having attained the limit
of the old year made me uneasy. It wasn't as though I were
walking out of prison.

Moira was hurt at my isolation. I could sense the crude
emotion run through her. It was abrasive. She said I was
selfish, that it showed in my attitude, on that of all nights.
I knew what she meant.

She felt the need to affirm something and in some way
or other she associated the possibility with the passing of
the old year. "Thank God this year's nearly over!" she
said.

That struck me as stupid so I didn't answer.

"Do you hear what I say?" she demanded.

I looked at her speculatively.

"Well?" she said.

She began to speak again but this time she broke off in
the middle. And then she walked across the room and

poured herself a drink. She moved from one event to another without ever coming to a decision. It was as though she were trapped outside her own experience, afraid to go in. I don't know what it was she was going to say. She poured herself a drink instead. I watched her from where I was sitting. Her thighs under the soft donkeybrown wool were attractive. She has still got good thighs. Her flesh is still firm and smooth to the touch; belly, buttocks, and thighs. The emotion was there, at all the muscle and fibre. And then she was opposite me again, sipping distastefully at her drink, avoiding my gaze. She was trying to give the impression that she was no longer aware of me and at the same time she sensed the absurdity of her position. That made her uncomfortable. For her the absurd was something to shun. She had a hard time of it, retreating like a Roman before Goths and Vandals.

It occurred to me that I might take her. She didn't suspect. She didn't realise her belly was more provocative when it had been run through with hatred. Hatred contracts; it knitted her thicknesses. She was hotter then, only then. As she began to doubt my love she became a martyr and unlovable. But anger sometimes freed her; her muscles had experienced excitement. . . . To walk across to her. She would pull herself up defensively and refuse to look at me. But her distance was unconvincing. She was not inviolable. That was the moment when I had to be in control of myself, for my lust tended to become acid in my mouth. I preferred her anger to her stupidity. It was something against which I could pit my lust. When I was confronted by her stupidity there took place in me a kind of dissociation, like the progressive separation in milk as it turns sour. I was no longer, as it were, intact, and she was no longer interesting.

I thought of the man in the lane. I had suddenly felt very close to myself, as though I were on the edge of a discovery. I was perplexed when I couldn't find him in the bar. I supposed he must have left while I was in the lavatory. The torso was cut deep in the wood, an oakleaf of varnish left where the pubic hairs were. I touched it with my forefinger, scratching varnish off with my fingernail. It struck me that it was too big. My wife had a big cunt with a lot of pubic hair, but not as big as that. It was heavily packed into her crotch. When I thought of it I always thought of it wet, the hairs close at the chalkwhite skin of her lower belly and embedded like filings in the pores. That made me think of her mother. I don't know why. The torso held my attention. I ran my fingers over it. The pads of my fingers were excited by the rough wood. I felt a slight prickling at the hairs at the back of my neck. I hadn't known wood so intimately before. I participated. I leaned against it. It felt good. That was when I first thought of my wife that night, more particularly, of the elaborate "V" of her sex, standing with my thighs close to the door, touching. I took one drink and left. There was no sign of any man. I looked up and down the street. I felt it was going to snow.

My memory of that New Year's Eve joins those two together, my ex-wife Moira, at her most abject, and the Glasgow proletarian my mother feared, and whose image in the lane under the gaslight, with a thing of silver in one hard hand, elides mysteriously into myself. I often thought it must have been a razor, Occam's perhaps.

It occurred to me she was wearing those new ear-rings her cousin brought her from Spain. That was the second time I noticed the ear-rings that night. She had had her ears pierced a month before. The doctor did it for her. She said she thought drop ear-rings suited her.

It was New Year's Eve. Moira felt she was about to step across a threshold. The ear-rings represented her decision to do so. The date was marked on a calendar. I had wondered why she was wearing them. She had said earlier she didn't want to go to a cinema. Actually I had forgotten the date. I was surprised she was wearing the ear-rings when I got back to the flat.

She was standing in the middle of the room, facing me. I felt she was waiting for me to say something. I had just come in. I was to notice the ear-rings. When I had done so we were to step hand in hand into a new calendar year. But I didn't notice them. I was still thinking of the man in the lane. And Moira herself got in the way, standing in the middle of the room, looking stupid, like she did in public when she thought no one was paying attention to her. Her eyes, as they say, expressed polite interest, indefatigably. At nothing, nothing. At the beginning I didn't see it. Perhaps it didn't exist at the beginning. I don't know. Anyway, it came to be as obtrusive as her mother's respectability. It had a murderous emphasis. As I say, I didn't see it at the beginning. I even looked the other way. But gradually it became clear to me that she was, among other things, stupid. A stupid bitch. And she had become a bor-

ing lay, unimaginative, like a gramophone. And so I didn't
notice the ear-rings and my foot was not poised with hers
on any threshold and my attention wandered.

I felt she was growing impatient, sitting there, nursing
her drink, that she was not sure whether to make a scene,
maintain her brittle composure there in the room, or go
out quietly. The last move alone would have been authentic . . . or if she had offered me a drink . . . but
she was incapable of making it. I think she thought she
gave the impression of being dangerous. But Moira was
never dangerous, or certainly wasn't at that time. She was
not in the least improbable. When the clock struck twelve
I heard chairs scraping across the floor of the flat above and
the muffled noise of a woman's laughter. When my wife
heard it . . . our chimes clock now continued its monot-
onous tick . . . she stiffened, and at that instant I caught
her eye. I had seldom seen her so angry. She lunged out
with her foot and kicked over the table. The whiskey
bottle splintered on the hearth and the whiskey seeped out
underneath the fender on to the carpet where it made a
dark stain. For a moment, contemplating it and then me,
she tottered like a skittle, and then, bursting into tears, she
threw herself out of the room. She had removed her body
with her anger. I felt suddenly quite empty.

My mind returned then to the lavatory. I had examined
the oakleaf and with my penknife I hewed it down to its
proper size. It was no bigger than a pea when I had finished, a minute isosceles triangle with a rough bottom edge
to it. I was pleased with the result. Leaning forward then
on the handle of my knife, I caused the small blade to sink

deeply into the wood at a low centre in the triangle. The knife came away with a small tug. The score, because of the camber of the blade, was most life-like; wedge-shaped, deep. I completed my toilet and returned to the bar. I drank a whiskey. When I left I made straight for the alley.

The flats above formed a tunnel over it where it met the street so that one looked through darkness towards light. Just beyond the darkness, half out of sight round a jutting cornerstone, the man should have stood. I walked along the centre of the lane through the tunnel. The lane, a dead-end, was deserted. The dustbins were already out. I lingered a while. Perhaps I was the stranger you watched apprehensively from your kitchen window. When I left the lane it was already dark and a lamplighter was coming in my direction with his long lighted pole.

The flash of silver . . . the sudden excitement that was almost a nausea . . . the thought of Moira before we left Glasgow . . . the whole complex of the past: I relived it all in that instant I caught sight of the man in the alley on my way back to the scow. The heroin had worn off but I was still pleasantly high from a joint that Tom and I had smoked on the way to Sheridan Square. The street was deserted. The man in the alley, facing the wall, hadn't noticed me yet. I was standing about ten yards from him. Like a man looking on a new continent. I felt the decision at my nostrils, and perhaps it was to communicate that to him, or perhaps it was simply to steady myself in my purpose—I lit a cigarette, cupping my hands over the match and holding them close to my face, causing the skin of my lower face to glow in the shaft of warmth from the match and leaving the skin about my lips tingling minutely in anticipation. The noise of the match striking and the sudden glow in the dark reached him. He froze momentarily and then looked sideways towards me. I could just make out the round yellowish face and the black moustache. There was a tightening pleasure at my entrails. I was quite sure of myself now. A nameless man. And something nameless had taken possession of me. I had simply to be and feel the workings of the nameless purpose in me, to grant, permissively to meet with, sensation unobstructed, rocked gently out of nightmare at him. He was buttoning up, slowly, it might have been reflectively, and then he turned towards me. There was something oblique and crablike in his movement. He was standing there, still under the electric lamp which shone on his shapeless double-breasted jacket at the shoulder and on the right side of his round face. I felt myself moving slowly towards him a foot at a time, looking straight at his face. It seemed that he moved forward to meet me. In a few sensational seconds my front was close to his front and our faces were an inch apart. I felt the warmth of his ear against mine and his hand. Belt, thighs, knees, chest, cheek. A few minutes later we were walking very close together back to my scow at Pier 72.

New Year's day. Early. Just after 2 a.m. I had just written:

> —My wife will enter as she made her exit, like a bad actor in a bad play, and when I move across to her she will make the gesture of resistance, for my act is her cue to resist; and her face will fix itself in its appallingly stupid lines and break where she smiles as she tumbles and says: "Don't Joe! You'll ladder my stocking!"
>
> She will not expect me to. So I shall catch her out at herself.

I heard them in the hall.

My wife's brother crossed the room after glancing at the shattered whiskey bottle. It still lay where she had thrown it. He was wearing a fawn cashmere coat with a thick blue and white scarf wrapped around his neck so that the head, tilted slightly backwards and bringing the fleshy chin into prominence, gave the impression of having been severed from the body and later cushioned there, neatly, pink, and vaguely apoplectic.

When he greeted me it sounded vaguely like a challenge. Robert was vaguely many things; a challenger, a man embarrassed, an inquisitor; his approach, his whole demeanour—at least towards me—was indirect. He was driven on by his sense of duty but was at the same time, so to speak, afraid to stir up the broth. He would gladly not have known what for a long time he had suspected. He had often said to me that he didn't think I was rotten through and through.

"Otherwise Moira wouldn't love you as she does, now, would she?" But it wasn't much after all. Not enough to dispel his consternation.

"Happy New Year, Joe!"

I took his proferred hand, thanked him, and wished him the same.

Moira, who had come in behind him, was staring angrily at the shattered bottle. Robert, turning towards her and following her gaze, murmured quietly: "Better clean it up, Moira. It'll get trod in."

She burst into tears.

"Now, now, Moira," Robert said to her, moving to her and guiding her by the arm towards the bedroom, "you just go to bed and get rested and let me talk this over with Joe." He followed her into the bedroom. I could hear him expostulating with her, imploring her to be reasonable. I felt sorry for him, for both of them, but I didn't think it was a good idea to go after them. It wouldn't have solved anything.

When he came back he sat down in a chair opposite me. He had taken off his coat and scarf. He held them on his knees as he spoke.

"You might have cleaned it up," he said.

"I probably will."

He nodded quickly and, after a moment's hesitation, he went on to say that he wasn't the type of person who interfered with other people's business, that if the war had taught him anything it was that there were two sides to every question. During the war my brother-in-law was a major in the Royal Corps of Signals. The military air, leavened by what I suppose he took to be his modesty, was to some extent still with him. He added that in his professional experience he had learned that it was not always useful to look at everything through one's own eyes; even the Law recognized this in its principle of arbitration, the judge in a Court of Law being neutral in spite of the fact that he was appointed by State. My brother-in-law was a solicitor. He often found it helpful to make a gesture to his authorities, military or judiciary, when he was leading up to his point, presenting credentials. He continued. He would be the first to agree if I objected to his arbitration on the ground that he was his sister's brother, and therefore not, strictly speaking, neutral. However, he hoped I knew *him*. And, as he had said before, he had no wish to interfere, especially as it was the New Year. He paused. He said he thought one should begin the New Year with a fresh start, not with recriminations. But there it was. Moira, he meant. The poor girl was deeply hurt. To throw bottles about, he meant. He knew I would see that. He had always known I was intelligent. And it wasn't like her to throw bottles about all over the place. We both knew that. He had said it. He had promised Moira he would have it out with me. And after all she *was* his sister. Very dear to him. He knew that she was dear to me also. He had never had any doubts about that. He would not say he didn't find me difficult to understand sometimes. A man who didn't work, he meant. Oh, he knew I was supposed to be writing or something. But after all I wasn't a child any more. A man of my age. Well, anyway, it was none of his business and the last thing he wanted to do was to interfere.

If Moira didn't mind working while I sat at home that was her business. But he didn't like to see her upset. It was the New Year. Bygones should be bygones. If I was agreed no more needed to be said. He was sure I would see things his way. I was a reasonable man. He was willing to shake hands and say no more. What now, agreed?

He allowed these last statements to fall on the silence as a grocer allows dried peas to fall from his brass scoop, one at a time, his head cocked, regarding the indicator needle fixedly, until it reaches the appropriate mark. I didn't mean to keep him waiting. Finally without saying anything I fetched the unbroken bottle of whiskey and poured him a drink.

"Happy New Year," I said.

"Happy New Year!"

We clinked glasses and he drank his down with obvious relief. Then he looked at his watch and said he had to be on his way. Claire was waiting for him. Claire. I always thought of Claire as strawberries and cream, cream, red and pink. He looked guilty for her. As well he might. She would have betrayed him for a dry Martini. She told him she didn't like me.

I helped him on with his coat and he wrapped the scarf round his neck. At the door we shook hands. As he left he turned back for a moment and said he was counting on me. I waved him down the stairs. Back in the room I finished my drink and smoked a cigarette. I might have laughed. But I always found it difficult to laugh alone.

> *Don't you suppose—since I am in a*
> *confidential and confessional vein—that*
> *when they have accused me of not*
> *being a good Spaniard I have often said*
> *to myself: "I am the only Spaniard! I*
> *—not these other men who were born*
> *and live in Spain."*
>
> —Unamuno

For a long time now I have felt that writing which is not ostensibly self-conscious is in a vital way inauthentic for our time. For our time—I think every statement should be dated. Which is another way of saying the same thing. I know of no young man who is not either an ignoramus or a fool who can take the old objective forms for granted. Is there no character in the book large enough to doubt the validity of the book itself?

For centuries we in the West have been dominated by the Aristotelian impulse to classify. It is no doubt because conventional classifications become part of prevailing economic structure that all real revolt is hastily fixed like a bright butterfly on a classificatory pin; the anti-play, *Godot*, being from one point of view unanswerable, is with all speed acclaimed "best-play-of-the-year"; anti-literature is rendered innocuous by granting it place in conventional histories of literature. The Shakespearean industry has little to do with Shakespeare. My friends will know what I mean when I say that I deplore our contemporary industrial writers. Let them dedicate a year to pinball and think again.

Question the noun; the present participles of the verb will look after themselves. Kafka proved that the Great Wall of China was impossible, it was a perpetual walling; that the burrow was impossible, it was a perpetual burrowing . . . etc. A "distance theory" of writing could allow for pockets of Stanislavski, of spontaneous prose.

Thus I take soundings. It's a complicated business this living it over again and apart from the forgotten judgments that were part of it. I am engaged in a complicated process of knitting, see myself as one of those old crones who during the Reign of Terror sat in the shadow of the guillotine as the heads fell, and knitted, on and on. Each time a head falls I drop a stitch, and from time to time I run out of wool and have to go off in search of a new ball. It's seldom easy to match colours.

Someone said somewhere that one doesn't marry a woman but an idea. That is rather imprecisely put, overstated. Still, it *isn't* very useful to suggest that we should go into marriage without preconceptions, go anywhere without them; if we hadn't such preconceptions we shouldn't think of marrying. I knew a very gentle and troubled Englishman who settled in Paris and married a dark, thin negress from Sierra Leone. She didn't speak English. She bore no resemblance to the romantic conception of *la belle negresse*. A fat, bluish purse of lips, a flat broad nose, eyeballs set outwards with the gleam of billiard balls, flat-breasted, thin-shins long on which rayon stockings hung loose and creased, making her legs look mauve, skin the colour of an eggplant, her taste in all things suggesting long indoctrination in a Mission School, her natural smell conveyed about her on waves of perpetually evaporating Eau de Cologne, her manner of sitting at the edge of a chair, tall, straight, with her hat on and wearing white gloves, her cheap navy-blue suit buttoned up to the demure white ruff at her neck, knees together, her feet ridiculous in Minnie Mouse shoes. When she visited she gave to whatever room the air of a waiting room in a provincial court. He read History at Oxford and not long after he arrived in Paris to study certain mediaeval legal texts he met her at a Communist Party "social" near Barbès. She had come with her sister and her brother-in-law. When she became pregnant he married her. He used to visit Moira and me when we lived together on the rue Jacob. He was in love with Moira in his quiet, hopeless way, and of all his friends we were the only ones who were permitted to meet his wife. I used to try to imagine conditions under which such a man would choose such a woman. For me she symbolized the vulgar triumph of all the tawdry goods, spiritual and material, which were foisted on the African in exchange for lands and freedom. *Ave Caesar! Nunc civicus romanus sum.* She was the kind of victim who believed it. Was it only later that he discovered this or did he know it from the beginning? Each time he visited us we could sense his reluctance to return to her, but he went always, and I have the impression that he is still doing so.

The idea which I married when I married Moira was
more obvious. From the age of twelve on she was the
princess of my immediate experience, first evidence that
beautiful girls existed beyond the shadowy, teasing images
of the cinema. Her beauty, I felt, would serve to put a
frame round my own which, sad to say, had up till that
time attracted the attention of few connoisseurs. I most
desperately needed evidence that in spite of the obvious
deficiencies of my birth I was, after all, a prince, and I
treasured intimations of things or imaginings to come as
jealously as a prospector his bag of samples. Daydreams
anyway, drained of all assurance each time I was confronted by Moira in the flesh, too struck and captivated by
her brilliant presence to have ulterior thoughts; indeed, I
had no more freedom than a yo-yo. Every dangerous act
of rebellion—in time I attained a relative mastery—was
consecrated to her, a classroom infested by six hundred
and forty-two bees, a fallen ceiling in the north wing, endless acts of sabotage to break the monotony of the long
school day. She was flattered by the grandeur of some of
these love tokens but remained out of reach.

My thoughts of her well beyond puberty were of a
ghastly purity. Softs and damps were taboo. If she had
dropped her pants I might have hanged myself. The first
time I noticed the new inscription in the boys' lavatory:
"Moira Taylor's cunt," I was stunned. Up till then my
romantic agony had prevented me from framing such a
concept.

The object of my wet dreams was another girl, the

highly sexed daughter of a Portuguese tart, whose actual
advances I was young and misinformed enough to consider improper. Sylvia. Her surname, like my own, provoked a strange response when it occurred in a list of more
native surnames: Laird, Little, Macleod, McDonald, Mor-
rison, Ross, Sylvia. . . . Sylvia Jesus Sylvia was the full
name inscribed in the register, and, in its shortened form
. . . Sylvia Sylvia, with the accent on the second syllable,
its sound was almost obscene; it trickled like olive oil
amongst the crags and the heather. She was reputed to
wear red knickers and her name was current in the school
lavatories. Although she was only a year younger than I
Sylvia was at three forms remove, considered a rather
backward child, a problem for the teachers because of her
abnormal physical development. Her academic placement
more or less cut her off from boys who, if she could have
attended their dances, might have been interested in her.

The school, a coeducational boarding establishment in
the countryside of Kirkudbrightshire—a brave, wartime
measure—was a sensitive spot for the more advanced edu-
cationists in Scotland. The many acres of garden and
park with its copses and wildlife in which children of both
sexes could wander was always a potential target for
the long moral rifles of the descendants of John Knox.

I was in the fifth form and had the privilege of visiting
the junior dance which ended at 7:30 p.m. After that,
Sylvia, as a junior, was not allowed in the large room where
the dances were held. Relations between her and me for
the rest of the evening were regarded as improper. The

headmistress, whose particular favourite among the boys I was—she saved me more than once from the wrath of the headmaster—was doubly hard on Sylvia.

"Sylvia Sylvia's cunt": I had no difficulty in conceiving that; I was conscious of its insistent animality every time I danced with her. On soft summer nights, set between her soft plump thighs, like a dark rose, it was served darkly to me in my dreams. I would promise myself that on the morrow I would say yes. But the sun rose with Moira Taylor and daylight defeated me.

I made love for the first time with a prostitute. Princes Street, Edinburgh. Ten shillings for a short time in an air-raid shelter. I had never seen such ugly thighs nor ever imagined it like that, exposed for me in matchlight, the flaccid buttocks like pale meat on the stone stairs, the baggy skirt raised as far as her navel and with spread knees making a cave of her crotch, the match flickering and this first sex shadowy and hanging colourless like a clot of spiderweb from the blunt butt of her mound. She rubbed spittle on it brusquely, as my mother with a handkerchief rubbed spittle against my cheek when we were visiting. She rubbed spittle on it and it was like someone scratching his head. It bristled then, and bared its pretty pink fangs. She told me to hurry up. The stone steps were cold. Above in the street there was a fine rain and I could hear the swish of tyres on the wet macadam. At my naked thighs I felt the night wind. The match was out. In the almost total obscurity of the shelter I lay on top of her and felt her belly sink cool and soft and clammy under my own.

I was a seaman in the Royal Navy at the time. I remem-

ber walking alone back to the Y.M.C.A. where I was staying. I went over it again and again in my mind, and by the
time I reached the Y.M. little feeling of guilt remained.
I was even in a vague way proud, callow possibly, but I
experienced an authentic feeling of relief. I savoured it
with a cup of milky coffee in the tearoom of the Y.M.

I had been lying in the bunk for over an hour allowing
thoughts of the past to mingle with my more immediate
memory of the man's naked body pressing down on me.
He had gone after about an hour, before dawn. I fell
asleep almost at once.

He was Puerto Rican and he told me his name was
Manuelo. He spoke almost no English and I almost no
Spanish and it had occurred to me as soon as we were in
the cabin with one kerosene lamp lit and the dead silence
broken only by the regular leak of water at the bilges of
the scow . . . on us and infesting us with its own secrecy
. . . it occurred to me that it was better that way. There
were no common memories between us; we shared our
male sex only, our humanity, and our lust.

It was not the first time I had had sexual experience with
a man, but it was the first time it was not in one way or
another abortive, it was the first time I had encountered a
man who knew how to take all that was given without a
trace either of embarrassment or of that shrill crustacean
humour dedicated homosexuals sometimes adopt, and my
body afterwards was heavy with the kind of satisfaction

I have often envied women. He drank a cup of coffee before he left, his lips smiling and his teeth very white under his small black moustache. "We see again? *Sí?*" he said quietly. I nodded and placed my hand gently on his. "*Espero, Manuelo,*" I said. He left shortly afterwards. And I went at once to bed to savour the intense satisfaction at my limbs.

I woke with all the sexual memories of my past, allowing them to come and go, comparing them, the reliefs, the triumphs, the shames. Occasionally I felt an edge of self-justification in my thoughts, a plea too intense, an enthusiasm caught up and too lugubriously rationalized, but I was fundamentally very calm and still profoundly satisfied, physically with the mute certainty of my body, intellectually because I had broken through another limit and found that I could love a man with the same sure passion that moved me to women generally. The river noises of the morning began to come to me where I lay smoking a cigarette.

. . . About ten in the morning someone knocked at the door. It was Irish, the market runner. He is responsible for the inspection of the boats and likes to be thought of as the "marine superintendent."

"Just a minute!"

I climbed off the bunk and got into my pants and a tee-shirt and went to the door.

"No up yet, man?" He was ramming tobacco into his pipe with his left forefinger.

"Yeah, got back late last night," I said.

"I thought you were on stand-by?"

I yawned and shook my head.

"Well look, now," he said. "I've just been down and looked below. Do you know you're carryin' more than a foot of water in them bilges?"

"Yeah, I think I must have sprung a new leak. I got a bad dunt from one of the Colonial tugs."

"When was that?"

"Oh, about a couple of weeks ago."

"Did you report it?"

Irish is a small man with tired angry blue eyes. I know he likes me but I could see he was displeased.

"There was no damage to report as far as I could see. It must just have loosened a couple of planks."

"Well, you'd better get down there and caulk it up, Joe. I'm going to leave the motor pump on the dock in about a quarter of an hour. So come and get it and get that water pumped out o' there, O.K.?"

I nodded.

His tone softened as it usually did after he had bawled me out. "I'd stay and help you," he said, looking at his watch, an inscribed timepiece from the president of the corporation, "but I've got to get over to Brooklyn. There's a bloody boat sinking over there. Bloody captain's gone ashore and can't be found."

"I'll get the water out, Irish."

"O.K. then, and remember always to report things, Joe. We can claim later then."

He went away, climbing laboriously over two other scows towards the dock.

—Shit, I thought, work. And Irish knew damn well it wasn't so easy to report something. If you put in a report you're putting in a report against the tug captain and you have to tell him at the time you're doing so. You are even supposed to get him to initial it. The tug captain can make life a misery for you in an hundred ways, or he can make it easy for you. So you don't put in a report if you can avoid doing so.

It was one of those unseasonal days of early February when the sun is shining and it seems as though spring has begun. The river seemed very broad and it was busy with slow-moving tankers, floating railway stock, and a wide assortment of tugs. The ferry from 42nd Street was moving like an old tramcar towards the Jersey shore. The water at the pier was filthy with all the refuse of the waterfront, rotting cork, food in varying degrees of decomposition, boxwood, condoms, all coated with scum and oil and dust. A man was working a pneumatic drill at the new heliport. I watched a few of the other captains go ashore. I would have gone myself after I had pumped out the bilges, but I was broke. —I must do that soon, I thought.

I got up from the bollard on which I had just sat down and returned to the cabin. It hadn't changed, but I was in the mood to notice things. As soon as I stepped across the threshold out of the bright winter sun it was into a dirty grey and white cabin which was for a split second un-

familiar, and a moment later, after my eyes had adjusted
themselves to the dimmer light, I sat down at the grey table
in front of cigarettes, matches, the dregs of a cup of coffee.
I opened the drawer and found the pill bottle in which I
kept my marijuana. I hesitated. It was not that there was
anything ominous in the thought of turning on; it was,
vaguely expressed, a feeling into the possibly profound
transition the drug represented, the transition in space, in
time, in consciousness. Whether it was nobler in the mind
to do what? And what kind of assassin was slung under the
belly of the sheep called nobler?

I looked at my pipe for a long time. It was an object over
which I had spent some creative hours. Moulded to the
bowl was a small bit of desert wood which I had painted
in the colours of heather and Scots glen. It was shaped like
an eagle with an extended wing and was hard and of intri-
cate lacquered surface interesting to close sight and touch.
It was a slim, long pipe and I should describe the workman-
ship as primitive Cellini.

As I filled the pipe I was already leaning over myself and
when I had smoked I was at the brink of an experience I
had already described in a note:

—It is as though I watched a robot living myself, watching, waiting, smiling, gesticulating, for as I prepare this
document I watch myself preparing it. I have stopped
at this moment, ten seconds? five? and the robot goes on
writing, recording, unmasking himself, and there are
two of us, the one who enters into the experience and
the one who, watching, assures his defeat. To look into

oneself endlessly is to be aware of what is discontinuous and null; it is to sever the I who is aware from the I of whom he is aware . . . and who is he? What is I doing in the third person? Identities, like the successive skins of onions, are shed, each as soon as it is contemplated; caught in the act of pretending to be conscious, they are seen, the confidence men.

I had that familiar feeling of regarding my whole life as leading up to that present moment before which I halted as before a kind of cosmic interrogation mark. At that moment I was at the mercy of whatever distraction, voices outside, the sound of footsteps, a hooting tug, the sense of my own shadow there in the cabin. It didn't seem to matter. Whatever increase of entropy in the external world, my response was relevant. The universe might shrink or expand. I would remain aware, a little pocket of coherence in the city of dreadful night. Or would I? The drug can be treacherous, leading through all the hollow recesses and caves of panic. An identity slips away and one can no longer choose to be immersed in it, voluptuously to be duped. I remember I was forced to lie down and close my eyes.

I was unable to return directly to my thoughts, whatever they were, and my former identity paled and disintegrated like the reflection of a receding face on the broken surface of water. If I had looked in a mirror and seen no reflection there I feel I wouldn't have been unduly startled. The invisible man. . . . For an indefinite time I existed as passively as a log, and on a correlative level of experience, as moving sap lives, darkly, in the veins of wood, and then, gradually or suddenly, later, I was involved in a spiritual excitement provoked by some object, still anonymous, out of the external world, and that naked excitement was both the occasion and the means of my denominating it XYZ to which I was forthwith committed. Thus an identity becomes, and his new created world.

Kafka said: "My doubts stand in a circle round every word, I see them before I see the word, but what then! I don't see the word at all, I invent it."

. . . Alone on the scows for long periods of time I sometimes find myself searching for topics to think about, or round, for although I enjoy the certainty of many discoveries, when my thought is like an engraving of tablets, there are moments . . . and the present is always suspect . . . when it is entirely frivolous, when, in barely connected sentences and unresolved paragraphs, I shit idiocy and wisdom, turd by turd, thinking impressionistically, aware of no valid final order to impose. Whatever I write is written deep into my own ignorance. And I find myself cultivating a certain crudity of expression, judging it to be essential to meaning, in a slick age vital to the efficacy of language.

It was still morning. At least I supposed so. It occurred to me that I was alone. And then it occurred to me how often that thought occurred to me. Sometimes it was as though I could only come to exist by writing it down on paper: —*I am sitting alone*. It had occurred to me that I was mad. To stare inwards. To be a hermit, even in company. To wish for the thousandth-making time for the strength to be alone and play. Immediately there was a flower on my brow, Cain's flower. To mean everything and for everything to be a confidence trick, tasting power coming into being for others; I had often thought that only through play could one taste that power safely, if dangerously, and that when the spirit of play died there was only murder. One could be in another's world anyway only indirectly; one had recourse to a kind of expression appropriate to that ambiguity, was masked always, even at the moment of discarding the mask, because for another the act of exposure stood equally in need of interpretation. . . .

As I lay there it occurred to me that my thoughts were becoming incoherent, which wasn't unusual. Sustained for a phrase or two, they splintered, and I imagined my mind as a kind of faulty lavatory system. It flushed unexpectedly and took some time to fill up. And one fill was pretty much identical to the next.

I began to think about Tom.

"*Go away,*" I said to the dog.

A growl came from somewhere near his palpitating underside. —Why, I thought, do I have to put up with this? The dog was just part of it, the last straw; when Tom relaxed and stopped bugging you . . . only on horse . . . the dog came in as an understudy.

In the junkie world there are many such last straws. One finds oneself of necessity giving the other man more latitude. There is no one whom Fay hasn't burned. But she continues to see everyone from time to time, when a man is desperate. Junkies in New York are often desperate. To be a junkie is to live in a madhouse. Laws, police forces, armies, mobs of indignant citizenry crying mad dog. We are perhaps the weakest minority which ever existed; forced into poverty, filth, squalor, without even the protection of a legitimate ghetto. There was never a wandering Jew who wandered farther than a junkie, without hope. Always moving. Eventually one must go where the junk is and one is never certain where the junk is, never sure that where the junk is is not the anteroom of the penitentiary. A Jew can stand up and say: "Yes, I am a Jew and these are my persecutors." There is always a possibility of effective resistance because there were always some gentiles who were not profoundly shocked when a Jew said: "It is not necessarily bad to be a Jew." Such tardy hope as is held out to junkies is that one day they will be regarded not as criminals but as "sick." When the A.M.A. wins the peonage will be less harsh, but the junkie, like the peon, will still have to buy at the commissary.

Thus there is a confederacy amongst users, loose, hysterical, traitorous, unstable, a tolerance that comes from the knowledge that it is very possible to arrive at the point where it is necessary to lie and cheat and steal, even from the friend who gave one one's last fix.

Tom loves his dog. He wrestles with it. It is for him the only being who doesn't present a threat. If it ever turns on him he can always kill it. It was the dog that decided me at one time that I couldn't live with him. It is an angry extension of himself, a weapon.

Except when we are under heroin our relationship is tense and unpredictable. It is only when I have fixed that I can forgive Tom everything, even the painful slowness, the hothouse movements of his fixing before me. Tom always fixes before me. He doesn't insist upon this. He simply observes a common ritual which I have always refused to observe.

Sometimes we make swift covert journeys at night through the backstreets of Harlem to cop. Tom has good contacts in Harlem and he likes to take me along. If you are a member of any underground in a hostile city it's good for one's morale. In the moonlight as we descend the dark stairs which lead downwards through a certain park I wait for him to say: "I go first."

I know that he will give me several moments in which to stake the prior claim and I doubt whether he's ever been convinced that I won't do so, even though I've said to him again and again that I don't give a damn who goes first once we're safely locked up in whatever pad and told him he gave me a pain in the ass when he carried on like that. I've waited for a long time for Tom to say: "You go first, Joe," but he never has and I doubt if he ever will. I have asked him why the ritual is so important to him. His answer is the usual one. "You never know when the Man will bust in. If they come, I want to have the shit in me." But that's not good enough. It's not always necessary to be a mouse, even if you're a junkie in New York. This kind of promiscuous creation of tension in a situation which is God knows far too intense already makes me very angry.

Unless I am in physical pain it is immaterial to me who

goes first. Tom pretends it isn't that way for him. He's lying. The urgency doesn't exist. To pretend that it does is to prostrate oneself hysterically before a malicious fiction. It is quite unlike the hysteria experienced by all of us in the day to day danger of our situation . . . (coming down the stairs at two o'clock in the morning on to the deserted subway platform at 125th Street, followed, it seems, by two unidentified men . . . don't panic . . . looking at us now from the other end of the platform . . . if they come within ten yards get rid of it). It is a submission to the very ignorance that has led to the branding of the junkie as a social menace.

"Dog," I said, "you're a mad dog. I know how you play. If I take that bone away from you you'll get real mad and bite. Who taught you to bite, dog? You know what happens in this world to dogs that bite?"

I don't know what it was that first attracted me to Tom unless it was that I felt him to be attracted to me. We just met, scored, and passed a few days together turning on. Most of my friends, especially those who don't use heroin, disliked him from the beginning, and I have often found myself rushing emotionally and intellectually to his defence. At times, after we had fixed and blown some pot, with a sleek thrust of my own soul, a thrust of empathy, I used to find myself identifying with him. I seldom do it now because Tom bores me nowadays, but I did so, often. But gradually I came to realize that he didn't think like I did, that he took my rationalizations too seriously or not seriously enough.

For example, he still talks about kicking, and at the same time he denies that he is hooked, and yet he has agreed with me again and again that if you simply put heroin down you are avoiding the issue. It isn't the horse, for all the melodramatic talk about withdrawal symptoms. It is the pale rider.

When Tom says: "I'm gonna kick," I say: "Bullshit." He becomes hurt and sullen. He feels I am deserting him. And I suppose I am.

He says he kicked before, the time he went to Lexington.

"Sure, and when you got back here you went straight up to Harlem and copped. A man doesn't kick, Tom. When he thinks in terms of kicking he's hooked. There are degrees of addiction, and the physical part has nothing to do with it. The physical bit comes soon and I suppose that then technically you're hooked. But with the right drugs you can kick that in a few days. The degrees of addiction that matter are psychological, like intellectually how long have you been a vegetable? Are you riding the horse or what? The trouble with you, Tom, is that you really put shit down. You use it most of the time, you dig it, but all the time you're putting it down, talking about kicking. It's not the shit that's got you hooked. You shelve the problem when you think in those terms. You talk all the time about copping and kicking. Talk about copping. Don't talk about kicking. Get high and relax. There are doctors, painters, lawyers on dope, and they can still func-

tion. The American people is on alcohol, and that's much
more deadly. An alcoholic can't function. You've got to
get up off your ass and stop believing their propaganda,
Tom. It's too much when the junkies themselves believe it.
They tell you it's the shit and most of the ignorant bastards
believe it themselves. It's a nice tangible cause for juvenile
delinquency. And it lets most people out because they're
alcoholics. There's an available pool of wasted-looking
bastards to stand trial as the corrupters of their children.
It provides the police with something to do, and as junkies
and potheads are relatively easy to apprehend because
they have to take so many chances to get hold of their
drugs, a heroic police can make spectacular arrests, lawyers
can do a brisk business, judges can make speeches, the big
pedlars can make a fortune, the tabloids can sell millions
of copies. John Citizen can sit back feeling exonerated and
watch evil get its deserts. That's the junk scene, man.
Everyone gets something out of it except the junkie. If
he's lucky he can creep round the corner and get a fix. But
it wasn't the junk that made him creep. You've got to sing
that from the rooftops!"

I have talked to him for hours. But in the end he always
comes back to saying he's going to kick. That's because he
hasn't really got much choice. He has no money. To get
money he has to kick and there's a fat chance of his kicking
without money. Still, it bugs me when he goes on talking
about kicking.

"I'm gonna kick."

"Man, you'll never kick." Sometimes I don't even say it.

"You bastard, I will."

"O.K. then, you'll kick."

"Sure I will. You think I can go on like this?"

"You did before."

"That's different. I was hung up then. I'll get the place fixed up good. You help me, Joe. If we only had some bread."

"How much rent do you owe?"

"Not much, a few months."

"How many months?"

"Must be about eight."

"You've been goofing for eight months? You owe $320 back rent."

"I'm gonna see him and say I'll pay it off, twenty a week."

"Where are you going to get twenty a week?"

"I can get a job. I'll start kicking tomorrow. I can kick it in three days. I haven't got a real habit. I'll get dollies. I know a stud who knows where to get them cheap. I'll stay off shit. I won't touch the damn stuff."

"Don't talk like an alcoholic."

But it's like telling a man inflicted with infantile paralysis to run a hundred yards. Without the stuff Tom's face takes on a strained expression; as the effect of the last fix wears off all grace dies within him. He becomes a dead thing. For him, ordinary consciousness is like a slow desert at the centre of his being; his emptiness is suffocating. He tries to drink, to think of women, to remain interested, but his expression becomes shifty. The one vital coil in him is the bitter knowledge that he can choose to fix again. I have watched him. At the beginning he's over-confident. He laughs too much. But soon he falls silent and hovers restlessly at the edge of a conversation, as though he were waiting for the void of the drugless present to be miraculously filled. (—*What would you do all day if you didn't have to look for a fix?*) He is like a child dying of boredom, waiting for promised relief, until his expression becomes sullen. Then, when his face takes on a disdainful expression, I know he has decided to go and look for a fix.

"You going to split, Tom?"

"Yeah, you comin'?"

I have gone with him sometimes.

"Look, you've still got some dollies, Tom."

"I finished them."

"Christ, already? O.K. I've got some goofballs and we can get a bottle of cough syrup. You can drink that."

"That stuff's no good."

"It'll cool you."

Two o'clock in the morning. Sitting in Jim Moore's drinking coffee slowly. A few haggard men. A drunk woman trying to get someone to go home with her.

"I'm going home, Tom."

"Where?"

"Bank Street. I'm going to try and get some sleep."

"Look, let me come with you. If I stay around here I'll meet someone and get turned on."

"I thought that's what we were sitting here for."

"No, Joe, it'll be O.K. tomorrow. It'll be three days."

"O.K. Come on then."

We get into the narrow bed and turn off the light. We lie awake for a while in the dark. I say: "Look, Tom, you'll be O.K."

"I think I can sleep."

I feel his arm move round me. I am suddenly very glad he is there.

I used to wonder if we would make love. Sometimes I felt we were on the brink of it. I think it occurred to both of us during those nights Tom slept with me in my single bed on Bank Street, his long brown arm round my body. There hasn't been much of what is ordinarily understood as sexuality in our relationship. The effect of heroin is to remove all physical urgency from the thought of sex. But on those nights we hadn't taken any heroin. We had drunk, turned on pot, taken whatever pills were available, and there were moments when our naked flesh touched and we were at the edge of some kind of release. If either of us had moved the other would probably have followed.

I can see Tom smiling as he comes in, his lips drawn back, showing his long teeth. He is wearing a chamois cap in the style of the English gentleman, a well-cut green pullover, drainpipe trousers, and a pair of oversized, beat-up ankle-boots. Over all he wears a brown leather coat of past days' motorists. When he turns on he walks and stands vaguely like an ape, bent at the knees, bent at the crotch, bent at the midriff, long arms dangling in front. Sometimes he carries an umbrella.

His first glance is at me, smiling across at me with his dark, beautiful eyes. And then, "Down boy! Down! Down, I tell yah! Christ, yah bad bitch!" The dog, its legs rigid, is dragged by the collar across the wooden floor and forced outside the main part of the loft. Tom closes the door quickly behind it, turns to me and grins again.

"You wanna get straight?"

He unbuckles his leather coat, hangs it carefully on a hanger, his cap on a hook, and unwraps the beautifully designed pale green scarf from his shoulders.

When I come with the water he is already pouring the powder from the transparent envelope into the spoon.

"I go first," he says.

I don't answer. I am watching how he lifts the water from the tumbler into the eye-dropper. I am wondering whether he is going to be quick or slow.

His nose is two inches above the spoon as he drops the water from the eye-dropper on to the powder. He holds the spoon near his eyes as he applies matches to it. He sets the spoon back on the table, bubbling.

He is doing all right.

Siphoning up the liquid again, applying the needle with its collar (a strip from the end of a dollar bill) to the neck of the dropper, twisting it on, resting the shot momentarily at the edge of the table while he ties up with the leather belt on his right arm . . . but I am already beyond all that. I am not watching and he is not playing for a public . . .

if he is I shan't notice because I am not watching . . . we
are both of us, I believe, relating each and separately to
the heroin before us. He is stroking the arm he is about to
puncture just above a blackish vein and I am already moving to cook up my own fix in the spoon. By the time I have
it prepared he is already loosening the belt. And now
he presses the bulb. It doesn't take long. It might have
taken much longer.

As I take my own fix I am looking at all the needle-
marks. They follow the length of the vein down the arm.
Since the Man looks for marks I am trying to keep them
dispersed, to keep them as impermanent as possible. Some
junkies use a woman's cosmetic to mask their marks; it is
simpler to stick to one vein until it collapses. They do so
and make up their arms, just where the elbow bends, like
a woman makes up her face. Shooting in places where the
vein is more submerged has over a period of time made
quite a mess of my arm. As I fix I am aware of Tom,
slightly to one side of me, standing, his left hand lying on
the table for balance, smiling idyllically. I wash out the
eye-dropper and sit down on the bed. I begin to scratch.

An hour later Tom says: "Man, that's good shit," and
he drapes himself at the other end of the bed. The dog
barks in the next room.

"Don't let the bastard in," I say.

I was still lying on the bunk at three in the afternoon
when Geo's scow was unexpectedly pulled in. I opened

the door and it was Geo, grinning hugely in greeting. "Runner told me to give you this," he said, handing me a letter. "I see it's from Scotland. Who's it from? Your old man?"

When I was four I fell from a swing and broke my arm. When it was set in plaster I asked for a big box with a lid on it, like the one the cat slept in. I put it in a corner near the fire in the kitchen and climbed into it and closed the lid. I lay for hours in the dark, hearing sounds, of my mother's moving about, of others coming and going from the kitchen, and inside sensing the heat of my own presence. I was not driven from my box until after my arm was healed, and then at my father's insistence. It was a stupid game, he said. And the box was in the way. A boy needed fresh air.

My mother was proud and my father was an unemployed musician with the name of an Italian.

The blue-black hairs on my father's legs gave to his flesh the whiteness of beeswax. I associated him with the odours of pomade and Sloan's Linament. The bathroom was his lair and his unguents were contained in a white cabinet affixed by four screws to a green wall. The pomade came in a squat jar with a red cap, the linament in a flat bottle on whose label was an engraved likeness of Joseph V. Stalin. Because of his strange moustache I always thought of Mr Sloan as an Italian. It was not until today that it occurred to me to suspect that he wasn't. The name of the maker of the pomade was Gilchrist, and yet it too was oily and glistened in my father's scalp.

In my father's obsequiousness there was an assurance,

but as he grew older he became reflective during the winter months. His step quickened, his distances were less ambitious. He spent more time in smokerooms over coffee and didn't move out again into the street until the waitresses had begun to sweep away the fag-ends which had been trodden into the carpet and to polish the glass tops on the tables. At that point he glanced at the clock he had been aware of since he came in, pretended to have found himself once again in time confronted by an overlooked appointment, and walked purposively to the swing doors. In one of his ungloved hands he carried a small leather briefcase which contained the morning paper, the evening paper, and a pale blue box of deckled notepaper with envelopes to match. Sometimes he stopped abruptly on the pavement and fingered the lapel of his heavy coat. He looked guiltily at the feet of the people who passed him on either side. And then he walked more slowly. Every so often, just in that way, he remembered his angina. The word stuck in his throat. He was afraid to die on the public thoroughfare.

Sunday. My father would be awake before the milk and the morning papers were delivered. He slept four or five hours at most. After the death of my mother he lived alone. At nine he shaved. Not before. The number of such necessary enterprises was very meagre. He had to spread them thinly over the day, as he spread the margarine thinly over his bread, to prevent the collapse of his world. The fort wall was a frail one between my father and his freedom. He shored it up daily by complex ordnance. He was chosen for by an old selector system of tested rites. He gargled, watching his eyes in the mirror. He polished his shoes. He prepared his breakfast. He shaved. After that he staved off chaos until he had purchased the morning paper. Births, marriages, and deaths. He moved up and down the columns at the edge of himself. But with the years he achieved skill. Either way he was safe. If none of the names meant anything to him he could enjoy relief; if a friend had died he could after that first flicker of triumph be involved in solemnity. His hours were lived in that way, against what was gratuitous, and he was all the time envious . . . at the brink. There is no suspicion so terrible as the vague and damning awareness that one was free to choose from the beginning.

Glasgow, 1949. When I let myself into his room my father was sitting in front of a one-bar electric fire. His hands were thrust forward in front of him, the fingers tilted upwards to catch the glow on his soft white palms. He was looking at the wedding ring of his dead wife which he always wore on the third finger of his left hand. He was pleased to see me. It was the first time since the New Year. He shook hands ceremoniously, holding mine within both of his, and then he lit the gas and put on the kettle. He said we would have a cup of tea. It was cold outside and he hadn't been out during the day. We were in for a long winter by the looks of things. He asked me if I was hungry. He had some tins, one of sardines, one of peas, and one of pilchards or herrings in tomato sauce—he didn't know

which. I said I wasn't but that I would take a cup of tea. He
nodded vaguely. "Damn gas," he said, "there's no pressure." He fiddled around with the rubber tube which was
attached to the gas-ring and then, still with his back towards me, he said: "Doing anything yet, son?" And I
said: "Not yet."

He leaned down and removed a piece of white fluff
from the carpet. For a moment he seemed to be at a loss
where to put it. He laid it at last in an ashtray on the
mantlepiece. His hand brushed the pale green alarm clock
which stood there and came to rest on his fountain pen,
which he carried in his right-hand vest pocket, fingering
it. He wasn't wearing his jacket.

When the kettle began to sing he came back again,
lifting the lid and peering inside. Steam rose up about his
hand. He replaced the lid, walked away again, and wiped
his hands on one of his very clean white towels. His towels
are always immaculate, especially the one he wears round
his neck as he shaves. He arranged it neatly on the towel
rail when he had finished. He said it was difficult these
days. The postwar boom was over.

My father had been unemployed for twenty-five years.

He stood well back from the teapot, his left hand
pressed against his paunch as he poured the water in with
his right hand. He was forced to lean down over the teapot to see if it was full. He poured the tea and handed me
my cup. As he did so, he looked hurt for some reason or
other, but he wasn't looking directly at me. "How's
Moira?" he said. "She back at work?"

I nodded. I asked him if he had seen Viola lately.

"Your cousin?"

He hadn't seen her but he had heard of her through Tina. Viola's husband was ill again evidently, one lung collapsed. He had given her a hard time; she had gone again to the minister as she would have gone to the priest. The minister talked to him, man to man.

"Still," my father said, "he gets a good pension. Your aunt's just the same as ever."

"I thought of going to see Viola," I said.

He nodded. "She'd appreciate it. She's had a hard time."

He looked at my empty cup and poured me another one, milk, sugar, tea, in that order. Then he sat, rubbed his stockinged feet, and put on his outdoor shoes. He supposed I'd be going in a few minutes. If I cared to wait while he put on a collar and tie he would have a drink with me before I caught the tram. He said again he hadn't been out during the day. It would do him good, he felt.

The beer was cold and almost flat. He introduced me to the barman. "Just down from the university," he said. Since I looked vaguely like a tramp both the barman and myself were a little taken aback, but upon my father's face there was a kind of waxen innocence, and no sign at all he was aware he was being inexact.

"What are you going to do now?" the barman said after a pause. He directed his question at me.

It was my father who answered.

"He's training to be a journalist," he said with a small, birdlike smile. He laid his finger at the deep hollow in his

temple. There was a macabre irrelevance in all he said.
But I was glad enough not to have to say anything. The
barman nodded his head, saying that the old days were
over, tentatively, and my father, his Adam's apple wobbling, tilted his head back to drain the beer from his glass.

"Have another?"

"If you're having one," he said.

"Two more," I said to the barman.

When they were placed before us I asked my father if
he wouldn't care to sit down. When we were in the company of a third person, whether it was a relative or a
stranger, my father had a trick of addressing himself to
him and discussing me as though I weren't present. In that
way, adroitly placing me in some sense beyond them both,
he was able at once to be proud of me and to cut the listener down to his own size; then, when my preeminence
was established, his little potato of a mouth split to show
a cheap crescent of false teeth, and he asked after the
other's offspring as though it were an old old story to
which he condescended to listen out of sympathy for the
other. From the point of view of the listener it was a disturbing game. If he was unskilful enough to attempt to
hit back, recounting the successes of his own offspring,
my father had only to glance at the clock, whistle soundlessly through his thin lips, smile tolerantly to give the
impression that he would have been interested if only the
subject had been more important, and say: "I don't want
to keep you late for that appointment, Joseph." Then,
with a small bow to the other, he would usher me away,

solicitous of my non-existent affairs. At this point, before we had gone two steps, he would play his ace. He turned round and said brightly to the other: "I'm sorry I've got to rush him away like this, but you'll probably have the opportunity of seeing him again before he leaves town. He's going to be here for a couple of weeks at least. . . ." The other, if he wasn't mortally offended, smiled weakly and nodded his head, for we were both looking at him, my father with an air of royal commiseration and I, forcedly, with one of polite and distant recognition. When we were alone again my father would be humming to himself, usually some light operatic air. After a pause he would ask me where I was going. If I was not doing anything in particular we could have a game of billiards.

I carried my beer over to one of the empty tables and he was forced to follow me with his own. I remember thinking that I shouldn't grudge the old man his victories, nor even his using me as a foil. They were more necessary to him than his bread.

He knew that he had displeased me and he laughed nervously when he sat down. "Good chap that," he said most treacherously of the barman.

"Tell me, dad, what does it feel like not to have worked for twenty-five years?"

"What? Pah . . . ha ha! that's not so! You're a joker, you are! Hem. . . . It's true I've been out of a regular job since the depression. Now, before that, son, as your brothers will tell you, you went off every year for two months' holiday, and all three of you were dressed in

white . . . not like your cousins . . . with bonnets to
match. Your mother wouldn't have you in anything but
white, and neither would I. Always out of a bandbox, you
children."

"But in a way it's an achievement, dad."

"What? what's that? What's an achievement, son?"

"Not working all that time."

"Pah, it's not true! I looked after the house! Who do
you think looked after the house? The house couldn't have
been run without me. Your mother was always too soft.
Good thing she had me!"

The reverse was true. He always made things twice as
difficult for my mother by generally getting in the way,
scaring the lodgers with his ugly temper, by bursting constantly into the kitchen like an angry bear and striking my
mother, or in one way or another reducing her to tears,
and by his habitual practice of seizing the bathroom and
barricading it against all comers.

A bathroom-toilet is a vital place in a boarding-house.
If one person monopolizes it a queer kind of consternation
overtakes the household. My father regarded the bathroom as his own.

He cleaned it and polished it and made every surface
gleam. He arranged the coarse runner-carpet lovingly as
though it were fine rare Persian. He waxed the oilcloth and
applied Brasso to the two inefficient carpet rods which
more or less kept the long strip of carpeting from gliding
into folds across the oilcloth when you walked on it. He
kept the windows spotless and changed the cream curtains

twice a week. (At the same time he grumbled if one of the lodgers wanted his curtains changed more than once a fortnight.)

He had four different locks on the bathroom door; a key, a snib, a snick, and a hook-and-eye. He used all four when he was in there himself, I suppose in all about eight to twelve hours a day. The kitchen was the family living-room, and my father and mother slept there in a retractable bed. All the other rooms except "the boys' bedroom" had been converted for the use of lodgers, so he had no other room of his own in his own house. The major cleaning took three hours every morning. It began as soon as the lodgers (by preference "professional men") went to work and the children had gone to school.

An old couple who came eventually to stay were the bane of my father's existence. The old man was crippled and had to be helped to the bathroom by his wife and my mother. Together they supported him across the hall and down the passage which led to the bathroom. On a good day their passage from the room to my father's lair took about three minutes each way. At the weekend the children often timed it and placed bets. A good passage was usually assured if my father was in a tolerable humour. Then he would stand with a peculiar, fawning smirk of distaste in the open kitchen doorway as the faltering procession passed, the old man wobbling on two sticks between the women. On a bad day the passage sometimes took as long as six minutes and was once clocked on a stop-watch at 6 min. 48 secs. This occurred almost exclusively cause my father was in a foul temper. The old couple visited the bathroom twice a day, once in mid-morning between 10:30 and 11:00, and in the evening between 7:30 and 8:00.

As the morning visit forced my father to interrupt his cleaning it was usually the more perilous. He would stamp and rage in the kitchen, shouting: "Always the bloody same! Got to clean the bloody place twice! Leave towels all over the bloody place!"

On such days the frail group quivered perceptibly as it neared the kitchen door. Then, when they had come and gone, my father would move with a cry of triumph like a beast to his lair. On bad days he was still cleaning the bathroom when those of us who came home for lunch returned. And then my mother would go nervous and angry to the door and knock on it: "Louis! Would you please finish up in there! Mr. Rusk wants to use the bathroom before he eats lunch!"

A cry of pained protest from my father. "Bloody people keeping me back! Can't get my bloody work done! Messing up the bloody toilet seat with powder!"

Sometimes he came out almost immediately and sometimes he lingered so long that my mother, with children and lodgers all clamouring to use the bathroom, had to go tearfully again to the door.

Every moment someone else was in the bathroom was an agony for my father. Even when he was eating (and he ate quickly, like a wolf) he kept one ear cocked for sounds from the bathroom next door.

"What the bloody hell was that! What's he doing in

there anyway? I thought he was going to eat his bloody lunch! When are you going to get a chance to eat yours, eh?"

"I've already eaten. Now eat your lunch and forget about Mr. Rusk." She was not convinced by his concern for her eating. She knew that as soon as the lodgers and the children had gone out again he would return to the bathroom and lock himself in until around five, professedly performing his own ablutions.

In the evening my father was out and in between baths, cursing the last visitor who had disarranged towels, who, if he were a child, had drawn "bloody silly faces" on the steam-clouded mirror. "Annie, will you come and see this pigstye!"

So when my father said with throaty conviction that the house couldn't have been run without him I grinned.

"I'm telling you the God's honest truth, son. Your poor mother was too soft. Everybody said that."

I laughed. "She was certainly too soft with you, dad. Now why don't you just admit it? You haven't worked for a quarter of a century. Now I'm not working either, so I'm following in your footsteps. You ought to be proud of me. When we meet one of your friends you should say: 'This is Joe, my youngest son. He's unemployed. Of course he's not quite up to his dad's standard yet because he's not unemployable, but I have great hopes for him because he's had a much better education than I ever got.'"

That amused him. "You're a devil, son!" He wagged his head. He became more serious. "But you'll have to make up your mind to do something soon."

"You didn't. That's the only difference . . . I knocked off a little earlier than you did. Strictly speaking, I never began. The trouble with you, dad, is that you've always been ashamed of being unemployed and so you never learned to enjoy your leisure. For God's sake, even when we were starving you wouldn't even collect the dole!"

"Queue up with that bloody tribe!"

"The proletariat?"

He smiled his little potato smile, distant, the better not to focus.

I went on: "You always pretended to be cleaning that bathroom of yours. That's what made you the bad-tempered rascal you were!"

"I kept that bathroom spotless," my father said rather gloomily.

"You want me to engrave that on your tombstone?"

"Don't talk like that, son."

"I'm not ashamed of you, dad."

"I know . . . I know. . . ." He had begun to whistle soundlessly in the abstracted way he had. He drank another beer and then he said he was tired.

"You won't come into town with me then?"

"No, I think I'll go to bed early tonight, son. I think I have a cold coming on."

I shook hands with him at the corner of the block where he lived. As he walked away I thought his room was always neat, the gas-ring cleaned with Vim and steel work. And "electric fires are not dirty. . . ." He eats one thin slice of bread with a cup of tea before retiring.

On the tramcar on the way home I wondered if it was

mere fantasy that I was reliving the life of my father, except that my attitude was different. I wondered whether I was kidding myself. I had just quarrelled with Moira. It was the same New Year.

> *The present is shored up by the past;*
> *and the not-yet, a void haunted by*
> *naked will, is too slickly furnished by*
> *the world's orators, like a harem in a*
> *Hollywood film, with no short hairs.*

"**R**ead it," Geo said. "But don't be long. I don't know when they're coming for me. I'm tied up at the other side of the pier. Come across as soon as you can."

He didn't need to tell me what for. It was one of Geo's peculiarities to turn up like that when you were least expecting him.

"I'll be over in five minutes."

"See you." He went out.

It was as though someone had just said: "You have won first prize in a lottery."

I opened the letter quickly. My father's spidery handwriting:

Dear Son,
    I was glad to learn that you are in the pink. Things have been going pretty slow with me. Philip says they

are going to start later this year and he won't be need-
ing me until July. I know things are not what they were
in the years immediately following the war but I do
hope he will find a place for his own Dad.

I am unhappy to say that your Aunt Hettie died last
week. Only your cousin, Hector, was there, both of the
girls being at Stranraer. Naturally young Hector
phoned me and I went along at once. I made some tea
but it was over very shortly. Young Hector said he had
been expecting it. You know your Aunt Hettie was
told to take it easy a long time ago. It was a great blow
to me, son. Since your mother died and then your Uncle
I visited her now and again and she was a good soul and
very good to me.

Hector is doing very well and very busy. He had to
stay off work the following day and make the arrange-
ments with the undertaker. I took him along and introduced him to old Urquart. You remember he buried
your mother? He's very reasonable and I have known
him since we were boys together.

Now son, there is no more news. I'll just have to hang
on as well as I can until July although they've finally
turned down my application for unemployment. It's
nothing but red tape and Philip is going to see what he
can do about it.

Hoping this finds you well. Best of Luck.

                                            Daddy.

I read it over twice and then dropped it in the table
drawer. I locked up the cabin, climbed on to the dock and
went to look for Geo's scow. I recognized it at once by the
emblem nailed to the mast. The bluebird of happiness,

Geo called it. He had painted a 16 oz. can white and on the white can he had painted the bluebird.

Geo was on the quarterdeck making up a dockline which was no longer in use.

"You go on in and I'll be in in a minute," he said. "It's on the ledge near the bed. You go ahead and cook up enough for both of us."

A bag of horse, a spoon, a dropper, a spike, and a book of matches. I was fixing when he came in. He locked the door behind him.

"Here, I'll clean it," he said, as I moved the empty dropper towards the glass of water.

I lit a cigarette, lay back against the bulkhead, and watched him fix.

"This is good stuff," he said, smiling down at the place where the needle was embedded in his arm.

"Just a minute," I said. I climbed off the bed, walked round him and across the kitchen to the bucket he used for a w.c. I vomited. It wasn't painful. It's not like getting sick on alcohol. The little food I had eaten during the day was soon regurgitated. Geo was standing beside me with a saucepan full of water.

"Here."

I drank and regurgitated, drank and regurgitated, the spasms lessening as whatever nervousness caused the nausea was neutralized first by the thought of my transcendent immunity, and then by the extreme but indefinable ecstasy at my senses. There was a wet, prickly sweat at my belly and thighs and temples. Geo thrust some kleenex into my hand. I thought of him as a saint and said: "Geo, what do

you think of Fay for an underground Florence Nightingale?"

"By the Marquis de Sade," he said. "She'd suck the fix
out of your ass."

The first time I saw Geo he was standing on top of the
load on his scow as the four tugs of the Cornell Sea Transport Corporation turned the tow on the river. There were
forty scows in the tow, four abreast, ten scows long. The
movement had already taken over half an hour because of
the state of the tide and the small winking light at the end
of the dark pier towards which we swung slowly was still
over fifty yards away. Beyond the pier and the riverside
streets the city rose up, the tall buildings, the Empire
State, Rockefeller Plaza, and the Chrysler building still
brightly lit with neon and floodlights. Advertising signs
flashed at both sides of the broad river: Lipton's Tea,
Cinzano Vermouth, Motoroil. The tugs hooted instructions at one another from time to time, moving busily
about, pushing and pulling at the tow. At that time of the
year there were a lot of mosquitoes about. As the scows
slewed round they droned at the shuttered windows of
the cabins and hung in clouds around all navigation lights.

Tugs of other companies were already standing by to
pick up some of the scows and deliver them farther afield.
None of the scowmen knew as yet who would go out that
night, and what conversation there had been during the
past half hour, shouted by shadowy figures across the

water from one scow to another, had been about who
would go straight out and who would remain at Pier 72
until next day. No one knew for certain. My own scow
was almost in the middle of the island of scows. I would
have nothing to do except let go my hawsers at the appropriate time. I was thinking of one thing only, the list. If
I was not on the list I would be able to go into the city.

"I hope I'm not on that fucking list!"

These were the first words I heard Geo Falk say. He
uttered them as he climbed down off his load on to the
short foredeck and stood, ready to let go a hawser, about
half-a-dozen yards away from me.

He told me afterwards that he was sick. It was on him
like something voluptuous, and at the back of his mind
a hedge of fear. It would be an oversimplification to say
that Geo was a masochist (any more than the rest of us),
but he did have a way of dramatizing his suffering, invest-
ing it with cosmic proportions, and the blood that trickled
down his arms was like the blood of the ten thousand fol-
lowers of Spartacus crucified along the Appian Way. If
he was pulled out at once he wouldn't get a fix. I could
imagine him becoming conscious of the cold set grin of
satisfaction at his jaws, a slave's defiance, and asking himself what the hell that was for and who he was trying to
con. I can see him standing on top of the load, his legs
apart and his hands on his hips, his blonde hair exposed to
the wind.

"Where you gaun?" another voice said in the dark.

It was the voice of a squarehead Swede. He was carrying
a flashlight at arm's length. It was on and its bright yellow

beam lit up the heavy gunwales of the scows as they swung closer together.

I watched Geo light a cigarette. "Port Jefferson," he said.

"You go out wid de tide most probable," the Swede said. "Day kom take you, I tink." He pointed to one of the tugs that was standing by.

I could imagine Geo muttering: "Fuck you!"

"Oh for me I doan giva damn," the Swede said. "I stay on de boat I save mawny. You go ashore you spend too moch an you drink an den you git broke. . . ."

Feeding Falk his damn squarehead philosophy.

I couldn't see either of their faces in the dark. I knew the Swede, but Falk I saw now for the first time.

"I gotta get off tonight," Falk was saying. He was speaking to himself.

"Ya, I tink you go straight out," the Swede said.

The bastard knows he's bugging him, I thought.

"You don't know a fucking thing," I said to the Swede. Falk glanced at me for the first time.

"You're Falk?" I said. "My name's Necchi. Fay told me to look out for you."

"Necchi? Yeah! Oh man, am I glad to see you! You hear the way that squarehead bastard's been bugging me? Turning the knife in the wound. You'd think he wanted me to go out tonight!" His laugh was high-pitched.

"I heard."

"Say, what's your scow? The Mulroy?"

"Yeah."

"Come over as soon as we tie up. Christ, I hope I don't

go out tonight! You know how far Port Jefferson is? I'll
croak if I don't get into town first!"

I had to go back to my bow. I nodded and left.

Neither of us were on the list. We went up to Harlem
together and copped some heroin. We turned on in a pad
up there, Jim's mother's pad. There was Jim, slim and dark,
who hadn't been clean for three years, Dulcie, his girl,
some trumpet-player I didn't know who was sitting on the
floor with his back against a wall, and Chuck Orlich.
Chuck was sprawled in a big chair, his arms dangling, his
tawny beard straggling on his chest, his shoulder-length
hair as voluminous as the wig of Judge Jeffries, and his
face was the kind of violet-grey colour faces have when
the organism is at the edge of death.

"Will you look at him?" Geo said. "Is he all right?"

"Man, you can't tell him anything," Jim said. "He takes
nothing for a week an then he comes here an takes an
overdose."

The shaggy head was thrown backwards, the mouth
open exposing stumps of teeth, a noise—click, click, click
—issued spasmodically from the throat.

"Naw, he'll come round," Dulcie said. "He's always
like that."

At that time Chuck was working in a wholesale
butcher's. He cleaned up all the bones and the blood after
the butchering. What a scene, the hairy Goth rummaging
amongst the bones . . . and the man was as gentle in his
demeanour as Saint Francis. Click, click, click—click,
click, click. . . .

He had come round before we left.

Next morning around nine we were pulled out together and during the next three days Geo and I were able to spend a lot of time in each other's company.

Geo was fed up with the scows. I was the only other man he could groove with. Some of them were O.K. but they were mostly alcoholics or men saving up to retire. He didn't want to die on the scows. He didn't want to die anywhere for that matter. But there was no other gig which paid so well for so little work. And no supervision. That was important. He often thought of Mexico where he had spent three years. The years in Guadalajara were Geo Falk's golden years. He had had money then, from the G.I. Bill. And at that time shit was cheap and plentiful in Mexico. (N.B. It isn't today.) Three years in the sun with plenty of horse, not too much, but enough, and he had painted. He hadn't really painted now for two years. Back in New York it was different. Without money and unable to sell any of his paintings he had been forced to push the drug to keep up his own habit. The girl he was living with finked on him and one day they came pushing him back into his room, treating him like cattle.

"O.K., Falk, we've come for you. Where is it? Where's your stash, knucklehead?" They didn't find the heroin but they found two spikes and with his marks and the girl's evidence that was enough. They built it up big for the tabloids so that John Citizen had the impression that Lucky Luciano's first lieutenant had been trapped by intrepid agents and that half the opium smuggled by Mongolian-faced agents of Chou-En-Lai from Communist China to sap the strength of the American People had been

seized in the raid; and in return for two Leica cameras they
played it down before the judge who, it must be assumed,
didn't read the tabloids.

Geo spent three months in the Tombs and when I met
him he was still on probation. He walked everywhere now
with a sense of his own criminality. Sometimes the Man
would stop him on the street and play with him.

"Howya doin, Geo? Still livin it up?" Flat eyes sizing
him up, lingering on his pockets, watching the set of his
hands; and his own inane smiling at the man who had arrested him.

"How about a drink, sergeant?"

And walking into the bar in front of him, his pride like
an insect struggling under a lethal weight, he heard his
own voice currying favour: "Feel much fitter now since
I kicked. Back on the old booze!"

"That so, Falk? I'm glad to hear that." And ten minutes
later. "Mind letting me see your arm, Falk?"

The time they put him in the Tombs he was in the cell
with a young Italian. Geo was in the bottom bunk. He was
lying with his eyes closed trying to steel himself against
nausea. The sobs of the Italian came to him and Falk found
himself hating him. Why didn't the bastard shut up? They
wouldn't give him anything, not even a wet cotton. For a
murderer yes, but not for a junkie, a junkie couldn't even
get an aspirin. Then he felt the wetness on the back of his
hand. What the hell? Jesus Christ! It was blood. Another
blob fell on the floor and splashed his hand. The Italian
was committing suicide. Call the Man. The Man took a
long time to come and when he came he said: "Why you

dirty little junkie bastard! What do you think this is, a pigstye?" They dragged him out, bleeding at both wrists. The door was closed and Geo was left alone with his mounting nausea.

If anything had broken him it was kicking his habit in the Tombs. When he thought of it he thought of destiny and he felt himself without will.

Geo is balding and he combs his blonde hair forwards, slightly oiled. His face has the battered look of an ex-boxer's. At thirty-three he is deteriorating; he is preoccupied with disappearing muscle. He watches, horrified, fascinated, the insectal movement of his private decay. And he massages the flesh which fascinates him with witch-hazel. Thinking brings a pained expression to his face and he is afraid.

We talked about how the world was just a conglomeration of rooms, other people's rooms, to wander about in. For ever and ever. For where our kind made a room the fuzz came, like something out of the movies, with drawn revolvers. It was like being at the mercy of a gang of belligerent children. We composed songs:

> *Where the buzz is*
> *there the fuzz is*
> *comin through the door.*
> *Where the fix is*
> *There the dix is*
> *comin through the floor.*

There was soon something between us. There were moments beyond all disbelief of good generosity. And I like the flaring of his paint, an abstract of Van Gogh's, but simpler. A yell in paint.

I returned to Geo's bed and lay down on it. The cabin of his scow is painted white and it always reminds me of an hospital room. Apart from his works . . . the big box of surgical cotton, the miscellaneous eye-droppers and needles . . . he has a vast supply of medicines, unguents, and disinfectants.

"I don't know why you don't do something about your damn cabin," I said.

"What's wrong with it?" He sounded surprised. "I just painted it." He grinned. "It's not finished. That white's the undercoat. But if I finished it I'd have nothing to do."

"I knew a guy once, Geo, who wanted to paint big. He used to sit in front of a pretty big canvas, 9 x 12, and it was already covered with size and white. He had a little room in a cheap hotel on the rue de Seine, near the river, and this thing on the easel used to be stuck out there in the middle of the floor like a screen and you were always walking round it and turning it and ducking under it. It was an object, anonymous, you know what I mean? And it was always intruding itself. And yet you were willing to play along with him and to accept his object and talk about it like I'm willing now to talk about the inside of your chickencoop."

"Don't stop," Geo said, grinning.

"That big white canvas must have been there for nearly

four weeks. I was staying with him at the time. I was camped on him, and when we ate or when we were spending time in the room for one reason or another we used to sit there and discuss what he should do next. He'd thought of putting a kind of orange splotch over half of it and we agreed we knew what he meant, not quite half, and not to make two oblongs like Mondrian might have, but just a splotch, like to surprise it. But although he'd thought of that he'd rejected the idea because he thought it might be too violent. He said he wanted the background to be tranquil whatever else he painted on the canvas. Well, he didn't do anything to it until one day we went to a Miró exhibition at the Galerie Maeght. There were a couple of really big canvases there, shape and colour objects against a great airy blue background. And the very next day when I came back from seeing a girl I was planning to make he grabbed me and screamed that it had come to him suddenly, just out of nowhere, and he dragged me round the easel to get a good look at it. He'd painted it blue, the whole thing, airy blue, just like Miró's. He was a small guy with black hair and he wore thick-lensed glasses. "It just came to me!" he kept on saying. "It just came to me!"

Geo, grinning, turned on the radio. To the tune of "Reuben Reuben I Been Thinking" a little girl's voice sang:

> *For a real treat this Thanksgiving*
> *Chock-lit turkeys sure are nice*
> *Get a chock-lit cross for Easter*
> *And for Criss-muss, chock-lit Christ!*

How can a man not write? How can a man not paint? How can a man not sing? But everything in measure. Let a man be measured, for there is no part of him greater than the whole man. Isn't it so?

There are times when I should allow a man to die beautifully, though in a man I expect self-consciousness, judging him less than a man if he is not, but granting his legal title still, which, without examining the heart of the matter, I accept at once on the level of prudence, which is also counselled to me.

Who speaks, knows not; who knows, speaks not.

Windy March and I make another beginning.

To bleed a stone. The anguish of this compulsion to record that swells beyond meaningful record. It is positively d.i.s.h.o.n.e.s.t. If I could find something to compel me equally. Marijuana has a tendency to set me against myself. My shadow waits for me, an instant of time in advance of me, and my knowledge of it can cause us to freeze into long abeyances. This practising of deceit against oneself, while it might be felt to be a waste of time, worse, perilous to one's integrity, is common knowledge to the wise. To live within one's imagination is brave, necessary; a man should know that the victims of his imagination can be many. The mass of men is afraid of imagination for this reason; with good reason, the tribunes will claim. Tell the tribunes that there can be no good reason for fear. It is fear that will destroy us.

113

The Eighth Avenue bus took me to 34th Street, the crosstown on 34th to Pier 72. The tug was already there and I boarded the Samuel B. Mulroy under a flood of insults from the tugboat captain. The scowman is the leper of the New York waterfront; he is old and can't work or he is a zombie who won't. The four scows linked together single file lay with the down tide from a corner of Pier 73 for three hours. Shortly after midnight the tug returned and the short slow haul down the Hudson to the stakeboat in Upper Bay began. Mine was the last scow and I sat aft at my open cabin door and watched the dark west waterfront of Manhattan slide away to the right. I thought of a night a long time ago when I had a girlfriend aboard for a short trip and how at the same kind of midnight we went naked over the end of a long tow, each in the hempen eye of a dockline, screaming sure and mad off Wall Street as the dark waves struck.

We arrived at Bronx Stakeboat Number 2 shortly after three in the morning and the tug, churning foam on the black water, backed away, its bell clanking instructions to the engine-room. She slewed round then and moved quickly away into the darkness. I watched her for a few minutes until the glow from her decklights dimmed and only the mastlights were visible. Then I entered the cabin.

A chair, a typewriter, a table, a single bed, a coal stove, a dresser, a cupboard, a man in a little wooden shack, two miles from the nearest land.

I remember feeling the night was going to be interminable.

I split a log and got the fire going. That helped . . . for a few moments, until I smoked a cigarette, stubbed it in an overflowing ashtray, and wondered what to do next. Even then, and all this is a long time ago now, I was no sooner alone than I would begin urgently to take stock.

I had come from London to New York and when I realized that the long affair between Moira and me was over I got a job on the scows. Time to think, to take stock. The grey table in front of me strewn with papers, inventories from the past, from Paris, from London, from Barcelona, notes neatly typed, notes deleted, affirmations, denials, sudden terrifying contradictions, a mass of evidence that I had been in abeyance, far out, unable to act, for a long time.

I wrote for example: "If I write: it is important to keep writing, it is to keep me writing. It is as though I find myself on a new planet, without a map, and having everything to learn. I have unlearned. I have become a stranger."

Seated at the grey table in front of cigarettes, matches, the dregs of a cup of tea. No radio. Dead silence broken only by dripping, on deck, at the windows, on the roof, in the bilges below. Sometimes the cabin shook in a gust of wind. And the sound of the bell came, giving me a sense of the emptiness of the night beyond the walls, and of the trackless water. For two hours I fought panic. I feared those moments and yet sometimes I felt a faint lust on me to live them again; and then I slid into a relentless movement which carried me again to the brink of hysteria.

It rained all night.

10 a.m. Samuel B. Mulroy, deck scow, bobs around on tide and currents, a low-slung coffin on the choppy grey water. The day is dull. The sky is low and greywhite. Tugs come and go, hauling linked scows, like toy boats playing dominoes. They come suddenly out of the mist which obscures Manhattan Island, hooting importantly. Leave two, take one. It goes on all the time the scows lie here. At the moment there are eleven of us strung out on wet ropes at the stakeboat. The stakeboat, which provides temporary moorings for scows on their way to unloading stages in Brooklyn and Newark, N.J., is uninhabited. It is an engineless hulk painted green and red and set with bollards, cleats, a winch, and a few hawsers. A painted wooden board identifies it as *Bronx Stakeboat No. 2*. The stakeboat swings about its anchors with the tide, the scows stranded out behind it in three rows, like beads on a string. Somewhere, not far off but invisible, a bell clanks dully and monotonously, a banshee wailing her dead. It comes from a marking buoy which flashes at night at regular intervals, a sudden explosion of white light which seems to hesitate before it occludes. And at night, if the mist rises, the lights on the lower end of Manhattan strike upwards out of the dark like an electric castle.

It was dawn when I went out on the catwalk.

The sun was struggling to break through a low mist and the surface of the water, glassy at this hour, was vaguely tinted with colour. I counted four scows behind me, a chain of three lying directly behind the stake, and, on the far side, three brick scows piled high with red bricks and

two yellow sand scows. This small shanty-town had come
to exist during the night.

The front scow of the centre chain is grey and red. It
is one of seventeen scows of a small sea transport corporation.

I sat on an upturned bucket at the stern on the port side
and gazed across the water towards the gradually appear-
ing Brooklyn waterfront. I had been drinking coffee all
night and I had smoked some marijuana. The smooth
water, grey-yellow, the tilting black cones of the distant
buoys, and the passing freight which moves slowly across
the estuary towards the North and East Rivers all contributed to the profound sense that came over me that I
was living out of time. It was cool on deck. I was waiting
to catch the junk boat which comes out to the moorings
from time to time to buy old ropes and to sell newspapers
and cigarettes.

Day. The rain is off. I am alone, suspended between land
and land, waiting to go with my load of grey stone to my
destination, *Colonial Sand and Stone*, Newark, N.J. I
watched dawn come near the open door of my little white
cabin, looking across the water at the extinguished sign of
Isthmian Lines, and I was wondering what I was doing,
doing just that.

It had been the same for years. The same situations.
Sometimes I thought I was learning something of my own
constructions. A scow on the Hudson, a basement room
in London, a tiny studio in Paris, a cheap hotel in Athens,
a dark room in Barcelona . . . and now I was living on a

moving object, every few days a new destination . . .
but always into the same situation. The voices, judging
and protesting, seemed familiar.

There was the Swede again.

It was around noon and I had been going to make a cup
of coffee but I was out of milk. Scow behind me was Harry
T. O'Reilly. I climbed up the short ladder on the bows on
to the load of stone chips. I like walking across a load. The
stones crunch under your feet as you walk the length of
the scow. There are 800 to 1,300 ton of crushed stone to
a load. A thread of thin grey smoke was coming from the
smokestack of the cabin at the stern. Get some sugar. Two
oil tankers were moving slowly towards the East River.
A helicopter hovered not far away. It was heading towards
Manhattan.

The Swede was using a handpump to clear his bilges of
water. He looked up as I approached. Broad face with
cropped grey hair, stocky, small blue eyes, and a thick red
neck. I'd forgotten it was his scow. He was a deep-sea man,
on the scows only until they were laid off for the winter,
he said. And then he'd ship out.

Another time I ran into him I made the mistake of accepting a cup of coffee. We had just begun the voyage
downriver from the quarry. I couldn't get rid of him all
day after that. He was always coming over to my scow on
one pretext or another.

"How ya doin?"

The man didn't read, not even a newspaper. He was always doing something with ropes or a hammer. The gallows carpenter of the Bothnian Gulf.

"How moch water ya got?"

He referred to the water which seeped in between the heavy planks and lay darkly like water under a pier in the bilges.

"Not much, I pumped her out yesterday."

He went away and I pretended to be engrossed in a newspaper. If it had been a book he would have asked me to tell him about it. "I no read moch bot you tell me, 'sgood?"

Five minutes later he was back.

"Ja, ya got seven inches . . . more. I measure. I thought yo tell me yo pomped?"

"Yeah."

"I bin down'n looked. What ya say I bring my pomp over, hey?"

"No, man. Just leave it, see? I like a bit of water for ballast."

"Ballast! Yo sink. Then it's not so fonny."

"O.K., sailor, but just leave it. I'm busy."

If he came with his pump he would be around for hours. It would break down. He would need my assistance to repair it. "Fon an games, hey?"

All afternoon he kept coming back. He spoke about women like a glutton might speak about pork chops (they were his enemies but he focked them), of one particularly whose legs he had broken in New Orleans. He described a frog crushed under a buffalo's weight. A white buffalo, a

skinny brown frog. "Sure I got de doc, de best, an he ask
me how dat happen, an I say hey hey you never mind how
it happen, doc, ya go ahead and fix it. I pay. Sure I pay.
Dat coss me fifteen hunred dollars! Tree hunred for de
doc an twelve hunred for de girl, hey hey! I gotta loak out!
I doan know my own strength!" He was grinning and his
big chest was expanded for inspection. "Ya shore ya doan
want dat pomp?"

I was surprised to see him using the handpump.
"What happened to your pump?" I said as I climbed
down on to the deck beside him.
"Yeah, dem bastards tuck it. Said I doan leak enough.
I quit. You see."
"I came to see if you had any milk."
"Milk? I got damn-ass all. I bin out tree fockin days. I
doan get ashore tomorrow I quit. I go down to New
Orleans'n get me a piece of ass."
"Break some more legs," I agreed. I was glad he didn't
have any milk. I didn't want him on my back.
A tug was approaching with three scows.
"Dey kom for me I tink," the Swede said.
They hadn't.
The tug came alongside and dropped off two of the
scows. I knew one of the scowmen, Bill Baker. His wife,
Jacqueline, was hanging some clothes on an outdoor line.
Her thick white legs tensed as she stretched upwards to
clip the pegs on.

I got some sugar from her.

As I went back to my own scow the Swede stopped me. He leered. I was aware of his forearms, heavy like two cods, and tattooed from wrist to elbow. His broad teeth were stained the colour of a neglected urinal.

"Hey," he said, "what yo mean about I break legs?" He looked dangerous.

"You said it."

"Ach, yeah . . . shore! But dat's all right. I pay. Shore, I remember. But I get me a big time down there in New Orleans. I not always like dis." He indicated his filthy sweatshirt. "I got seven new suits, eight wid the one I got before, smart, de best material, an I got a 1955 Buick convertible. Dem clothe coss me near a tausen dallar. I go there I have all the ass I want." He hesitated and nodded in the direction of the woman who had returned to her chore. "Nat like her," he said. "All I want. Yong pussy. I wouldn' toch her wid a goddam pole, heh, heh!" He grinned. "Yo kom mit me, yo see!"

I made my way for'ard, ignoring his restraining gesture. In my own cabin again I had just lit a joint when he knocked at the door. I stubbed the joint and dropped it in the table drawer. He stood in the doorway, one hand on the portal, leaning there.

He said: "Yah! Sa great contry Amerika! People kom here! You take de Poles or de Germans, or even de English. And dere's de Irish too . . . I like de Irish, dey's good people . . . hey, hey, yo lok what de English done to dem, heh? Dey all kom here. Man worrks, he git paid, de bess monney in de worrld, an hey! man free to go where he want, nut like de Rooskies. Dey got anodder tink kommin to dem, dem Rooskies, yah! Dat Eisenwhore knows what he doin, yo see. Yah! here in Amerika yo got de great mixture. All kom here. Too many wops maybe. An dere's de niggers. I'm not for to discriminate against any man'n here in Amerika dey's all equal, dass de law. . . ."

"Yeah, big deal," I said. "Now look, Swede, I want to read."

"Yo read too moch," he said, and he burst out laughing and tapped his close-clipped skull with his broad fore-finger. "Yo read too moch yo get sick op here!"

"Yeah," I said, "book-learning. Now, fuck off!"

When he had gone I found I'd got sugar instead of milk. I didn't want to disturb Jacqueline again so I drank my coffee black.

I smoked the rest of the joint.

It was nearly dusk when I went on deck again. A small boat was pulling away towards Brooklyn with Bill aboard. He was seated at the stern, beside the man who handled the outboard.

"Where's he off to?" I spoke to a scowman who stood on his quarterdeck near by.

"His son's in trouble."

"His wife not go?"

"Her! Na. Not her son." He spat in the water and went into his cabin.

A wind had sprung up. The water, a few feet away, was the colour of oiled slate and growing darker. Dark clouds overhead. It felt like rain. A fast ripple was spreading over the water like a dark jingling mirror towards the distance of Manhattan Island, small and black, like jutting granite rock. The water choppy, dangerous. Most of the men had already hung out their lanterns which swayed and creaked at the swaying masts.

I hung my own lanterns and returned to the cabin.

I must have decided to smoke some pot because I found myself lying on my bed with my pipe in my mouth. I was staring at the bulkhead on which the corpses of the previous summer's insects were encrusted.

Experts agree that marijuana has no aphrodisiac effect, and in this as in a large percentage of their judgments they are entirely wrong. If one is sexually bent, if it occurs to one that it would be pleasant to make love, the judicious use of the drug will stimulate the desire and heighten the pleasure immeasurably, for it is perhaps the principal effect of marijuana to take one more intensely into whatever experience. I should recommend its use in schools to make the pleasures of poetry, art, and music available to pupils who, to the terrible detriment of our civilization, are congenitally or by infection insensitive to symbolic expression. It provokes a more sensual (or aesthetic) kind of concentration, a detailed articulation of minute areas, an ability to adopt play postures. What can be more relevant in the act of love?

Sensation, being the raw material with which any probable metaphysic must contend, a hypocritical attitude to-

wards it can be disastrous. In the Middle Ages the passion-
ate love of a man's own wife was reckoned to be adultery.
In the modern world all attachments which are not to the
state are coming to be regarded as at least frivolous. While
the mediaeval Church couldn't burn every heretic, it is just
possible that the modern state can, even without recourse
to the atomic bomb. Before we give up any sensual pleasure
we should have explored it thoroughly, at least in sympa-
thetic imagination; otherwise, history moving forward
primly on its moral bicycle (in morals, nothing as complicated as the internal combustion engine has been invented)
may leave something primal and essential behind.

These, more or less, were the thoughts which came and
went as my mind moved ineluctably towards the deserted
woman from whom I had borrowed sugar. Gradually, as
my mind began to dwell on her, thoughts were replaced
by images and images by premonitions of sense.

I had known Bill ever since I got the job on the scows.
A man around fifty, he had that kind of tawny, greying
hair which reminds one of pepper and salt. His eyes were
pale blue, his short straight nose had some kind of growth
upon it at the left nostril, and his thin lips, drawn tautly
downwards on the left side, gave to his expression a perma-
nent air of disbelief. We had towed together a number of
times and we had often exchanged remarks about the
weather. His wife had attracted me from the beginning.

It came over me gradually that she was beautiful. A
vague shock. She was taller than average, her body loosely
knit yet oddly graceful. Her face gave the impression of
being archetypal, ageless, the face of a young clown. Her

soft brown hair was twisted in an untidy tail at the nape of
her neck and a few stray wisps—I often had the impression
that she had just washed the upper part of her body—still
wet, dark featherflecks, clung to the pale skin of her
shoulders. Usually she wore a man's collarless shirt stuffed
at the waist into a pair of faded and tattered blue jeans.
Her eyes were brilliant, clear, luminous, grey-green, the
gaze almost hypnotic, and sometimes I had found it difficult to tear my own eyes away from them. At such times
I felt the impulse to step close to her and take her in my
arms, as though only she and I existed, the rest background,
out of focus, expressing without speech and through a
sudden perfection of my whole organism the nullity of
everything else.

Sometimes she shrugged her expressive shoulders and
looked at you in a wide-eyed, limpid way. Sometimes she
seemed to have come right out of a daydream, a strange,
wild creature, almost like Medusa.

I spoke of her thick white legs and I was aware of being
inexact at the time, for of course she was wearing jeans.

As she hung up the clothes she stood on the balls of her
feet, foot, I should say, for she had only one leg. The other
one was artificial. It came to you all of a sudden as you
watched her limping movement, the way she stretched,
the way her hips swayed to find balance. As she stepped
back from the line, the clothes pegged and fluttering, she
almost toppled into the water, and as she saw me she
laughed. She sat down on the heavy beam above the
gunwale, stuck out her lower lip and made a wry face.
Sitting there in her blue jeans and the collarless, smocklike

shirt, her soft hair untidy, her face was not exactly elfin, and yet it was. She had the long shallow nose of a young witch, very high cheekbones, vast, delicate mauve eye-sockets in which her large green eyes, long-lashed, out-lined and elongated boldly with a dark pencil, took on a look that was haunted, not quite of this world. She used no colour on her lips. Her teeth were yellowish and looked fragile, almost like a rodent's. The bones of her shoulders had a birdlike delicacy, and there was something winglike about the way she used them. She had a long, pale, yellow neck whose length was exaggerated by her collarless shirts, and she had long, pale, white arms.

She got in the way of my request and I asked her for sugar instead of milk.

I went outside in the dusk but it was too windy to linger on deck. I returned to the cabin. Through the window I saw a light approaching across the water and wondered for a while if it was a tug. It soon veered away to starboard and moved into the distance. It began to rain.

I suddenly became conscious that I was trying to avoid thinking of the woman. So I began to think of her. Her image fled. I began to verbalize. Tallish, lanky, soft front. Breasts. Three nipples, one extra to give the devil suck. My reaction to the leg that wasn't there. Creak, creak, creak as she walked, swinging her wooden leg. Only the pink stump, like a withering tuber. So near her cunt. Remove the man's shirt. The chest almost hollow and the breasts falling like two soft things, close together, towards her navel. The body like pale ivory. Ageless. About 23? And the clownface. She didn't need more than one leg.

Although comings and goings between the scows were infrequent, a small and temporary shanty town formed there every night between dusk and dawn, about two miles off the southern point of Manhattan Island at Battery Park. More than a dozen scows huddled together, a wooden island beleaguered during that night by driving rain.

I put on my oilskin and sou'wester and stepped out on to the quarterdeck. The water was sliding away fast beyond the anchor chain of the stakeboat. It was quite dark, only the dim lights from the lanterns at the masts and the pale oblongs of light from the cabin windows. It wasn't likely I would meet anyone on the way. Because of the foul weather most of the scowmen would be in for the night.

I walked quickly along the load of the scow behind my own, crossed the quarterdeck of another to reach the third chain, and climbed up the side of another load. A dog barked somewhere nearby and a gruff voice cursed it. Across the beam of my flashlight the rain fell in long silver needles. I moved forward, my shoulders hunched to bring the rim of the sou'wester well over my neck.

It wasn't too late to go back. What would I say to her? My mind was inoculated against every objection. I was telling myself over and over again: "You have nothing to lose."

I reached the quarterdeck and walked round to the cabin door. There was a light on inside. That was the one thing I had been afraid of. If she had been asleep I couldn't have woken her up.

I drew a deep breath and knocked sharply on the door.

Noise of stirrings inside. A chair scraped across the floor.
The sound of her walk. "Who's there? What is it?" The
door opened a few inches and she stared out at me. "Oh!
It's you?"

"Can I come in for a minute?" The rain had somewhat
dampened my style. I couldn't think of anything else to
say.

She opened the door and allowed me to step in. She was
dressed as usual. The cabin was stuffy, dirty, and, if possible, more dismal than my own. There was a shelf of well-
fingered paperbacks near the large double bed on which
a rumpled and patched red bedspread had been thrown.
The stove, crowded, it seemed, with dirty pots, had been
painted a shiny black and the two small rooms with no
dividing door were lit by two battered kerosene lamps.

"The lamp in there's smoking." It saved me from saying
anything else for the moment. I pointed.

A tremulous black thread of oil-smoke was suspended
between the scorched globe and a spot on the bulkhead
where the fine particles of soot densened and wavered in
a flat, spider-like cloud, while the globe itself, a chancre of
red and yellow and black in suppuration, shed less and less
light on the objects in the bedroom.

"So it is!"

She moved quickly and turned down the flame. I took
advantage of the delay to loosen the coat at my neck.

"Listen to that rain," she said as she came back. "What
do you want?" she said. "Are you out of sugar again?"
She was smiling, her lips barely apart and turned up puck-
ishly at the corners, her mouth a dark elliptical slot.

"As a matter of fact I made a mistake this morning," I said. "It was milk I wanted but I asked you for sugar."

"You looked distracted," she said.

"Did I?"

"Sure. You nearly always do. Bill talks about it all the time. He calls you the absent-minded professor."

"Do I look like a professor?"

"I didn't say it. He did. At the moment you look like wet soap. Take your things off. You might as well now you've come all this way. I'll make you a cup of coffee, with milk."

"Thanks."

I took them off and sat down by the table and lit a cigarette.

"When do you expect him back?" I said.

"Oh. . . ." She turned to look at me. "How'd you know he was gone?"

"I saw him go in the boat," I said.

"I don't know. He said he'd try and get back tonight. But I don't know now. It's getting pretty rough. There's no rush for the load evidently. They're going to leave us here until he gets back."

"He won't come tonight now."

"No. Probably not."

She must know, I was thinking. In many subtle ways Jake and I—her nickname, short for Jacqueline—had already and even explicitly reacted towards one another. Nothing had been said and yet the bond between us was explicit. Or so it had seemed to me. Now I began to wonder. Was it all inside my own skull?

"So you came because you knew he wasn't here?"

There was no anger in her voice. Her tone was permissive and curious. And so I hadn't been mistaken.

"Yes. That's why I came."

"O.K. I guess it had to happen some time."

"I was hoping that was how you felt."

She carried over two cups of coffee.

"Well, it is," she said. And she laughed again. "You picked a fine night!"

"Bill picked it," I said. "Anyway, I'm glad I came."

"I kind of like it, the rain I mean. It isolates us. Makes you feel the rest of the world can go to hell."

I laughed. "It's probably radioactive. That's the trouble with the external world. It keeps impinging on you."

"I'm glad you came, Joe. I was feeling pretty low. God it can be hell marooned out here!"

"What about Bill's son?"

"He was still on probation. I don't know what he did this time."

We sat in silence for a while. And then she began to tell me how she lost her leg in a car accident, how they had amputated above the knee. She said her hair had been blonde before that, but she said it idly, in passing.

We talked for hours, the ambiguous presence of rain and night silence seeming to hold us closer together within the small wooden shack. I must have talked incessantly about myself, about how I didn't really want to do anything, about how, even if I still wrote, and used to think of myself as a writer, I didn't any longer, how I thought of myself as a man with nothing to do in the world ever, except to remain conscious, and that was what the writing was for, for my own use and the use of my friends. I told her that the great urgency for literature was that it should for once and for all accomplish its dying, that it wasn't that writing shouldn't be written, but that a man should annihilate prescriptions of all past form in his own soul, refuse to consider what he wrote in terms of literature, judge it solely in terms of his living. The spirit alone mattered.

I told her how the war had in a sense clinched matters for me, about air-raid warnings on the east coast of England, how I and the other recruits were made to run on the double from the barracks to the air-raid shelter, how we ran down the long stone corridors of the training ship and over scabrous dark ground near the cliff to the brick entrances, and then down the concrete steps into the narrow underground passages to the nearest wooden bench, there to sit, elbows on knees, an illicit cigarette cupped in our hands, waiting away hours for the all clear. All during the war no bomb had been dropped within miles. Naturally. The bombers were more interested in civilians. But night after night, haggard from lack of sleep, we streamed obediently into the burrows, and at six o'clock in the morning, an hour after the all clear sounded, we formed squads on the parade ground. We were dressed, turned about, stood at ease, called to attention; we were shouted at, marched, and run at the double in long lines. And sometimes we did the slow march like they do for the dead. At seven we fell out to fall in to eat breakfast. We fell in outside the dining hall according to messes and fell out of a long single file to eat our mash. Afterwards we fell in.

I told her that the first six weeks of training finished me,
how I spent the remaining three and a half years in the
lavatories of various training ships, armed with a long-
handled broom so that I could pretend to be scrubbing the
floor if anyone important came in; my best trick, for it
never occurred to anyone that a man would impersonate
a lavatory cleaner. I did most of my reading there, Plato,
Shakespeare, Marx, and I masturbated myself thin. I never
saw the enemy until after the war and that was in Norway
from whose King Haakon I had a red, white, and blue
certificate thanking me for liberating his country.

She said she felt exactly as I did, like being unwilling to
commit herself to anything, ever. She didn't want to do
anything, travel a bit perhaps, just be, have a child maybe,
but simply have it and let it grow up with her.

"Bill thinks we haven't got enough bread. He thinks I'm
irresponsible. But we can get bread without making the
kind of scene he wants to make. He wants to buy a motel.
I've had an abortion before. I don't want another one."

The atmosphere had become conspiratorial. She went on
talking and her voice grew soft and I sensed her nearness.
She was no longer talking about Bill, but about the present
moment, all present moments, about us really, not com-
plaining any longer.

We sat talking for another hour or so. I found myself
taking her hand and when we got used to that feeling, the
vast sense of possibility touch implied, she extinguished the
oil lamp. As we lay down on the bed I heard her draw in
her breath. She smelled sweet and warm. The other lamp
was still burning, but low, and it gave off almost no light

because of the soot on the globe. I moved my hand over her buttocks and she moved her stump between my thighs and pressed her belly close to me.

Afterwards, as we lay in each other's arms beneath the rough blanket, the sides of her belly and her flanks were covered in a thin lather of sweat. We breathed in and out together and flesh fell away, leaving a slight prickle on the skin. It was still raining. We could hear its fall on the water, on the gravel load, on the wood of the deck. It was there with our breathing, something objective to which we both listened as, with our eyes open, and with our own thoughts, we looked at each other in the dark.

At the age of five I walked with my elder brother to school, along grey streets in a sprawling grey city; on my back a little burden I was to carry through life with me, a cheap leather bag with shoulder straps to carry knowledge in. Cold pink thumbs in the straps of my schoolbag, lifting their cutting weight off my collar-bones, against the weight of books and into the driving sleet. A pain in the nose in search of an identity.

Aunt Hettie dead. She was the first woman I ever saw naked. She slept in the cavity bed in her kitchen. One afternoon I went in and she was alone, standing naked in the middle of the floor. I surprised her in a pose that she would subsequently have to explain to herself.

I was sixteen, her favourite nephew. She was about fifty at the time, with grey, almost white, hair. But the hair on her mound wasn't grey. It was the colour of a hazelnut.

She was angry at me for barging in unannounced. She was a little drunk. But she calmed down, put on a dressing gown, and made tea. We sat in front of the fire. She said in her husky chain-smoker's voice that I would be making women dance "bare-nekit" soon enough.

When I was younger I was afraid to kiss her. The skin of her face was porous and she was old and smelled of port and soiled underwear. But that day my attitude changed.

The house was empty, she was naked, and I was nearly seventeen and deadly curious.

"Where's Hector?" I said.

"He just went round the corner. He'll be back in a few minutes."

We sat in silence, each conscious of the other in a new and disturbing way.

That night I stayed at my aunt's, sleeping with my cousin Hector. In bed I contemplated the possibility with vague lust before I went to sleep. Hector was sleeping soundly and I could hear my aunt moving around in the kitchen. But at the last minute, standing outside the kitchen door in the dark hall, listening, breathing softly, I lost my nerve. I'm inclined to think that I knew I would from the beginning, that I knew I should not have the nerve, that the satisfaction I sought was in the danger of the dark passage, naked in the hall. Anyway, I didn't go in, and afterwards I didn't say anything to Hector, a boy a year younger than I. It was his mother and I thought he might be angry.

Two factors combined to give the impression that my aunt was fat. Her paunch had spread with middle age. Her cheap, fitted skirt made an inverted pear of her lower torso. Then, she wore no brassière, and her large, pendulous breasts were slung within the stained woollen jumper like a bag of meat almost at the level of her navel. When she moved about, her broad Slavic countenance sailed under a bell of grey hair. Or she sat, feet on the hob, her knees up and causing her thighs to fall like Gladstone bags below the hem of her skirt. Seated like this, a smouldering cigarette at her lips, she shot spittle or fart at the fire, drank tea or port, and directed the complex prenuptials of two unmarried daughters who in their later teens were groped and punctured on the couch in the parlour. Christ died there nightly on wood hewn at Jerusalem, and Elvira, a dead member, was pale within the mahogany frame to which memory and a cancerous tumour had transposed her.

It was my father's opinion that his brother's house was unclean.

From time to time, in a variety of places, my mind has travelled back to the dead Elvira, to the couch whose old springs creaked under human weight, to the silver photograph frame containing snapshots of my uncle in Naples, in Jaffa, in Suez. He died eventually of coronary thrombosis, the disease which killed my grandfather. In our family, amongst the menfolk, it is the heart which cracks first.

There were many visitors at the house of my aunt. The sex of two young females, and, in their absence, the various articles of a personal spoor, was the catalytic influence which governed the confluence of things, of the stewing meat, of the bottle of ruby port secreted beneath the disordered cavity bed, of teacups accepted and discarded by the perpetual stream of visitors who came there in the afternoons and in the evenings and late at night when the girls appeared in the kitchen with their smoking rumps and ate Finnan haddock which their father, retired from the sea and working as a chef on the trains, had carried south from Aberdeen.

The girls, now women of mature age, were Viola and Tina.

I remember Viola in her petticoat at the sink. Her mauve armpits glistened with soap. She sponged, and the suds returned to the tin basin where her hand was. The small spike of wet hair down which the water trickled was at that time eight years old and the armpit itself was twenty-two. The hair spread electrically while she was still in the convent about the time of the first flowering of the bloody roses. Her bodily beauty got her a professional man against whom at moments of extreme tension she still invokes the Church. Malcolm was a medical student not yet qualified. They lived in obscure furnished rooms at the east side of the city. She conceived for the first time defiantly, in squalor, and since that time, because her husband became a semi-invalid, her rooms have always been more or less obscure, and her attitude has been one of tearful defiance, more or less. As a child I was always in love with Viola.

Each time I saw Angus he was going to or coming from bed. He was an argumentative man of slow speech and a score of rocklike abstractions. When those were not questioned his utterances began, broke, or ended with a yawn, and were often inspired by the weather. This last fact was strange because he had been on the night-shift in a factory for fourteen years and the subtleties of the weather were for him little more than a memory. "It's cold," he said, or, "It's hot," or, sometimes, "It's raining." The other was most helpful when he commented on the state of the weather during the day. Angus narrowed his grey eyes and rubbed his prominent Adam's apple. It was pale, pointed, and bony, like the joint of a plucked chicken's wing. If there was any discrepancy between the item of information furnished by the other and the meteorological report on the radio Angus became reflective. If the other man was still with him, he posed a question, his voice deliberate and high-pitched: "You said it rained all day?" The other nodded hesitantly. "That's funny," Angus said. "It said on the wireless it was showery with bright periods."

The other sister, Tina, was married to Angus and she copulated with him on Sunday mornings after reading the Sunday newspapers. That was in the bed behind the green curtains in the parlour where under the photograph of Elvira, Tina's piano had stood since she became a woman of property. She owned a small general store which remained open sixteen hours a day including Sundays. It was hard after her father succumbed to coronary thrombosis, for in his latter years he worked only six days a week in the kitchen of a large canteen and was thus free to work in the general store on the seventh.

"He should've told us!" Aunt Hettie said after the last spasm.

There was a time when Tina was merely not beautiful. After she got goitre I visited her in the private nursing home where she had carried her shame, her boiled-egg eyes and humped throat, amidst a litter of hairpins, chocolate wrappings, filter-tipped cigarettes, and ailing females, each in a sad way excited to be a victim amongst other victims and to indulge herself in toilet waters and expensive bed-wraps such as that kind of invalid carries to that kind of place. Each was strangely flushed, with fats arranged nicely under silks and cashmere, and emitting an ambiguous odour of scents, illness, and sweat. They were very fond of the nurses.

Tina is out now and about, but her eyes at odd moments slip silently out of alignment and she has the aspect of looking at the floor and the ceiling at the same time. When she remembers, she wears dark glasses, but she likes to be told that they are not necessary.

Hector, my boyhood friend, is the youngest member of the family. After his return from the army of occupation in Germany he worked as a commercial traveller. Like most of the younger salesmen, he was only "marking time." But after a few months Hector brought to the most obscure mysteries his eye of a commercial traveller. No other eye was his to bring.

It all seems a long time ago now, and my father saying his brother's house was just a bloody railway station.

5 a.m.   Tug came for three of us before midnight. We moved line ahead over the dark water past Brooklyn towards Coney Island. My scow was at the stern of the tow. The ferris wheel was still alight. I felt rather than saw activity there as we drew nearer. Faint sounds. Suddenly round the point on our starboard side the unutterable night of the Atlantic, big, black, and menacing; there was no more light from the Jersey coast. From now until we gained the lee of Rockaway Point we were in open sea.

I'd heard about it from some of the other scowmen but I hadn't thought much about it, how a flat-bottomed scow loaded down almost to the gunwales with a thousand ton of stone, and slung in a chain of scows behind a tug, moves when it is suddenly struck broadside by the black Atlantic.

It struck me as funny tonight that it should take place

off Coney Island in sight of the ferris wheel and all that crazy-motion machinery.

I had blown a joint and I was brewing a cup of coffee in the cabin when it struck. Somehow the helmsman of the tug misjudged his distance as he rounded a marking buoy and caused it to leap like a wild top between the linking lines of the tow. First I heard a sharp crack from somewhere up at the bows and then there was an unidentifiable scraping or gouging which seemed to approach my cabin with the shuddering noise of an express train. I moved quickly and as I opened the door an anonymous object like a huge Chianti bottle rose out of the spray, toppled quick and ghostly around my port quarter and hurled its way out of sight into the swirling trough of water astern. I was still wondering what the hell that was as I became aware of the Atlantic rising like a sheet of black ink high on my starboard and blotting out even the night sky.

I was standing in the wind, clutching at the doorway of my shack, the sea falling steeply away under my narrow catwalk, and for a moment I had the impression of tottering at the night edge of a flat world. Then I was going down like you go down on a rollercoaster, braced in the doorway, the cabin light flooding out round about me as though it would project me into the oncoming blackness. Black, then indigo as the horizon moved down like a sleek shutter from somewhere high above and flashed below the level of my eyes. A moment later the sea rose with a sucking sound and slid like a monstrous lip on to my quarter-deck about my ankles. It was icy cold. At that moment, staring down at it as it swirled round about the battened hatches, it occurred to me that I might be about to die.

It is surprising how after that split-second hesitation as one becomes adjusted to that possibility one moves at once to prevent it.

I had the sense of being adrift.

I locked the cabin door and climbed on to the roof where my storm lantern was creaking and dancing like a gibbet. Staring for'ard over the load it seemed to me that the long shadow of my own scow and that of the scow ahead were bending together in the night like a gigantic hinge.

I moved gingerly on the leeside along a lifeline towards the bows. I knew as I got there that my starboard hawser was gone and as I climbed round on to the fo'c'sle I saw that both crosslines had gone too. That left my port hawser. When that went, without power, my scow would be so much flotsam in the Atlantic. This had just occurred to me when the man on the scow ahead, the devil himself it seemed to me at that moment, an ageless taciturn German with a beard and wearing a sou'wester, struck two blows with a heavy axe and parted my port hawser.

I think I might have screamed, at least a dying curse, when a lighter line, his one remaining dockline, came snaking across my bows. I moved at once, aware in a side-glance of the yawning distance between my scow and his, and thrust the eye of his line over my bollard amidships. I signalled frantically that it was secure and watched him stumble backwards with the free end of the line. He took a few quick (or slow) turns around his own port bollard and prepared to check it out slowly. I knew now what he was up to. You can't control a single hawser manually in

rough weather. If my last hawser had remained unparted
we might have collided as castanets do on a short string.
That anyway is the theory upon which he was prepared
to risk casting me adrift. I clung to the capstan and
watched him prepare himself for an unknown shock. At
the instant at which the rope became taut anything could
happen. Fishermen know about this. The moment at
which the rope takes the strain is the dangerpoint. Check
too strongly and the line will snap. Check too generously
and a fish will run away with the longest line. I calculated
that (if he hadn't sold some to a junkman to buy lush) he
still had about thirty feet of dockline to play with, and I
felt that was very little for a give-and-take between two
monsters on a rough sea. The tautening rope with spray
darting from it emitted a dangerous singing sound which
came to me by a strange species of sensory selection above
all the other noises of wood, wind, and sea. The first
abrasive retch of the rope at his bollard and I knew that
the rope was now running like a quick snake through his
gloved hands.

"—Take another fucking turn!"

I think he did so, for I could see now he was bracing
himself. I watched him pay out a few more feet of line, and
then he was checking hard, paying it out inch by inch. But
I knew there couldn't be much of it left. Not much of his
line left, after which I in my weighted coffin would drift
off alone into the night.

I thought of preparing a line of my own, but it was
pointless. I could only make out the vague shadow of his

stern now and I couldn't have thrown it that far in the wind.

I became aware again of the Atlantic, big, black and endless, and wished to hell I'd had a fix. If I'd had a fix in the cabin I think I would have struggled back along the lifeline. I hope the fucking tug knows what's happened back here, I thought. I was still clinging to the capstan, shivering in a tee-shirt and shorts, and then, as suddenly as the first noise, I felt myself picked out like a wet insect by a searchlight.

Another tug was moving swiftly alongside.

A laconic voice came through a megaphone:

"What d'you use for hawsers aboard that boat of yours, Mac? Your brassiere?"

I watched a deckhand throw a line skilfully over my port bollard. I looked at the bridge: "Fuck you, egghead!" I screamed.

There is no story to tell.

I am unfortunately not concerned with the events which led up to this or that. If I were my task would be simpler. Details would take their meaning from their relation to the end and could be expanded or contracted, chosen or rejected, in terms of how they contributed to it. In all this, there is no it, and there is no startling fact or sensational event to which the mass of detail in which I find myself from day to day wallowing can be related. Thus I must go on from day to day accumulating, blindly following this or that train of thought, each in itself possessed of no more implication than a flower or a spring breeze or a molehill or a falling star or the cackle of geese. No beginning, no middle, no end. This is the impasse which a serious man must enter and from which only the simple-minded can retreat. Perhaps there is no harm in telling a few stories, dropping a few turds along the way, but they can only be tidbits to hook the unsuspecting with as I coax them into the endless tundra which is all there is to be explored. God knows it's a big enough confidence trick to make someone listen to you as you gabble on without pretending to explain how Bella got her bum burnt. I said to myself: "Well now, here's a nice barren wilderness for you to sport and gambol in, with no premisses and no conclusions, with no way in and no way out, and with nary a trail for the eye to see. What more can a man want to fill his obscene horizons?" Drainage trouble in your home? Drainage trouble? A stopped-up sewer may be to blame. I drank a bottle of cough syrup (4 fluid oz., morphine content ⅛ grain per fluid oz.) and took a couple of dexies and felt better. Nothing like a short snifter to buck you up when you find yourself near Perth Amboy, New Jersey, sitting on the handpump on the port quarter of your scow whose starboard side is swinging just free of the docks, and the dung-coloured water sliding away smoothly, horizontally, before your eye. On it, a tanker. Beyond it, and to either side of it, low brown and green countryside, low bridges, concrete piles, elevated roads with automobiles like little ladybirds running across them, and squat and strutted things, trucks, gas-tanks, telegraph poles, scows, gravel, endless concrete, low, flat, dispersed, representing, dear reader, man's functional rape of unenviable countryside, marginal flat and bogland. As the afternoon wore on the sky was becoming thin and milky-white and the water gleamed blankly in reflection. To walk beyond it all would have taken how long, one pillbox after another through the skeleton factory, mile after mile flat and deserted? The nearest bar, I was told by the last dockhand before they knocked off, was just over a mile away beyond that underpass; that the first evidence that man was not only a working animal, and yet really not much more than a filling station between there and the next bar a mile farther on, and so on, and so on. It reminded me of the North Sea in a fog, of Hull or Sheerness, places like that on the east coast of England.

I left the scow after dark around 10:30 and walked through a brickyard to reach the path leading up to the road. I walked slowly along a single railway track overgrown with weeds and found myself amongst brick kilns like the kind of sandcastles you make by inverting a child's sandpail. The furnaces of two of the kilns were going full blast, casting a red glow which threw my shadow in black on the wet gravel. —I am walking through hell or Auschwitz, I thought. And then the dreary climb up beyond the underpass. It was spitting rain.

It took me an hour and a half by bus, ferry, and subway to reach the Village. I bumped into Jody in MacDougal Street. We walked towards Sheridan Square. Jody was wearing blue jeans and a cheap, imitation-leather jacket, powder blue in colour. Someone gave it to her. She disliked it but it was at least warm and all her own clothes, so she had told me, were locked away in two suitcases, impounded by some landlady uptown to whom she owed rent.

As we approached the lights of the intersection her hand

went automatically to her hair. It was fine brown hair, cut short and close at the ears, and cut short like that it made her finely chiseled features look hard and sculpted. This impression was intensified by the wide sweep of her plucked eyebrows and by the mockery which came often into her beautiful pale brown eyes.

She lived with a girl called Pat who loved her and paid the rent. That was Jody's way. Jody's share of the rent, if she could have brought herself to pay anything, would have been less than the price of staying high for a day. But for some reason or other Jody never paid. She invented excuses. She had lost it. It had been stolen. She had been burned. Pat was a square, a lush . . . why pay her anything? And if it wasn't Pat it was someone else, even myself at times, and Jody could always find a word to cap her victim and justify the unseemly executions. There was the time she took $20 from me to cop and didn't return until the following evening high out of her mind with a fullblown story of a big bust and shit flushed down toilets and arm inspections and Malayan elephants and she had been lucky to get away at all. (Not just one little taste for me, Jody? *The iris closing*. You hang me up for twenty-four hours waiting for shit, you come back zonked and expect me to think it's lucky you got back without it? Aw, Joe, I couldn't help it, honest. Let's blow some pot, Joe, just you and me . . . I didn't burn you, Joe, honest . . . I told you it was a bust, honest . . .)

I met her first through Geo. I was staying at Moira's place. Moira had gone away for a fortnight. The blinds were drawn all the time. I scarcely left the apartment. It was a time of fixing and waiting and being and fixing and waiting. Jody made all the runs. She had a good contact. She came with Geo and when he left she stayed, like some object he found too heavy to carry away. How do you do, Jody? It seems you're living with me. The atmosphere became much less tense the morning Geo left to return to his scow. Jody asked me if I would like a cup of coffee. And she went out and brought back some milk and a few cakes. Jody loved cakes. She loved cakes and horse and all the varieties of soda pop. I knew what she meant. Some things surprised me at first, the way for example she stood for hours like a bird in the middle of the room with her head tucked in at her breast and her arms like drooping wings. At first this grated on me, for it meant the presence of an element unresolved in the absolute stability created by the heroin. She swayed as she stood, dangerous as Pisa. But she never fell and I soon got used to it and even found it attractive. One time she turned blue and I carried her over to the bed and massaged her scalp. She came round almost at once. It might have been the increase of circulation in her head. Or it might have been the fact that Jody didn't like anyone to touch her hair, or indeed, any other part of her. She was always at the mirror, arranging her hair. It had to be perfect, that and her makeup. Sometimes when she was high she would spend as much as an hour in front of the bathroom mirror.

"Does it never occur to you that you spend a helluva time each day in front of a mirror?"

She was immediately, you might say understandably, on the defensive. A shadow crossed her face, the secret closing of the iris.

Her skin and her colour suggested delicate, fragile china. The clearly marked eyebrows, the finely curved cheek, and the dark, accentuated beauty of the eyes, heightened this masklike effect. Her lips were dull, soft, red, hard, full; the nose aquiline, curved smoothly and sharply, like all the other aspects of her face. Her pupils were often pinned and shadowy, her delicate nostrils tense.

In a way she was always abstracted. I have described a beautiful face, but the beauty was not at all conventional. In fact there were moments . . . when she was stoned in the flesh and tired by the use of too many drugs, by too little sleep, by a hard coil of inner desperation which caused a certain latent vulgarity that was hers to come to the surface . . . when she looked cheap and ugly. Below the mask then a stupid confusion was evident. It showed in her whole manner, particularly in the nervous move- ment of her hand arranging her hair, a movement which was indistinguishable from the fatuous gesture a cheap whore might make as she stood up, caught sight of herself in a wall mirror, and prepared a face to leave the bar with.

Like many part-time hustlers she had had many affairs with other women. They always ended in the same way. The other woman did the hustling. When Pat had an accident and was taken to hospital Jody didn't budge from the apartment. "I hate sick people," she said. Pat sent Jody money from the hospital. When Pat came out she was confined to bed. "She thought I'd take care of her,

Jesus! I'd be readin and she'd *want* somethin! She always *wanted* somethin!"

We crossed Seventh Avenue and went into Jim Moore's.

"She comes on with this baby stuff," Jody said. "Jo-dee! It makes me sick. Always buggin me!"

"What did you do?"

"I ignored her. Then she got mad an said she paid the rent. I asked her what that had to do with it. She thought she'd *bought* me! Can you imagine that? You broke your leg, I said. I didn't. If you didn't get so damn lushed it wouldn't've happened. I wouldn't take the blame for anythin, nothin!" Jody said. She pulled her coffee to her and drank some as soon as it arrived. She put sugar into it and asked for some more jelly with her English muffin. "She screamed herself sick all day an next day she moved out. She went to stay with a friend till her leg was better."

I burst out laughing.

The way Jody said it was funny. But that wasn't what I was laughing at, although she was under the impression it was and burst out laughing in delight at my response. And her delight was no less affecting because it was, in a logical sense, mistakenly triggered. Spontaneous laughter is infectious and draws people together. And I had laughed first and found myself effectively delighting in her delight. The words, even their meanings, were in a sense superfluous. I remember wondering at that, how the fact of laughing together nullified the inauthenticity. Even now it is with a feeling of generosity that I remember what I laughed at then, which was the memory of her own pathetic indignation when someone up in Harlem burned

her—"The bastard! After all I've done for him! When he
had no bread I used to turn him on!"—about that, and the
self-criticism her hard talk about Pat implied, for like
people generally, Jody, no matter what she was talking
about, talked exclusively about herself. I used to wonder
whether she knew it.

When we had finished our coffee and when no one we
knew had come along . . . we were looking for loot to
score with . . . we crossed West 4th to the Cote d'Or.
We pushed in through the swing doors. The place was
crowded, dark as usual, the bar on the left and the single
row of tables on the right. The first thing you noticed was
the exhibition of paintings along two walls just below the
ceiling. At that time they changed them every so often, but
soon it was just a bar again with a mixed clientele. I didn't
go there much by that time because it was one of the few
places I was fingered. I had been waiting for Fay, drinking
a beer, and I had been spotted by the barmen as one who
was more interested in dope than in drink. That's a bad
thing in any bar, and barmen are quick to notice. Most
barmen are very indignant about drugs. Still, one of the
barmen had been in Paris and most of his customers were
very friendly towards me. It's true that Fay was as loud
as a white feather in wartime; if anyone ever looked like
a junkie, she did. With her unkempt hair, her fur coat, and
her blue face, she moved ferret-like into a noisy barcrowd
and out again. I have seen many a drunken face frozen,
the lower jaw dropping, to follow Fay with the eyes out
of the bar. Fay and I left together and hadn't gone much
more than a block when we were suddenly grasped from

behind and thrust roughly into the entrance hall of a small block of flats. A strange coolness descended on me as soon as I felt the hands; in my imagination I was already saying to the policeman: "And now be on your way, sir. You have no business with me." And then I was looking at them. Middle-sized, they were dressed in leather lumber-jackets and looked like competitors in the *Tour de France*. They were flashing some kind of identity cards which evidently convinced me. It hadn't occurred to me that they could be anybody else. They were straight out of Kafka. And yet I knew they were real beer. I don't know whether they were members of the Federal Bureau of Investigation or of the Internal Revenue Service, but they were very ugly in their anonymity and very impertinent. Fay seemed to know them well and immediately adopted a doglike attitude towards them. She wagged her tail. Tongue and saliva drooled from her mouth in friendly effervescence. I found myself against the wall with one of the bicyclists ordering me to turn out my pockets. My passport would stop him for a bit. Ten years of border-crossing had furnished me with impressive documents. I was carrying some bennies, but I wasn't worried about my vulnerability. I was worried about Fay's. In fact she knew far more about these men than I did, having met them before. But I was a foreigner and might be deported very easily. Fay could expose more with less danger than I. As I slowly and absentmindedly emptied my pockets, I ignored the man who was examining me and kept interrupting Fay's interrogator.

"You stay outa this!"

"Look. I kicked. I'm clean, I tell yah!" Fay repeated.

"Can't you see she's telling the truth?"

"Look, who are you, mister? Didn't I tell you to stay outa this?"

They didn't find anything on us and Fay was shooting in her hand and not in her arm at that time. They didn't look at her hand and fortunately they didn't look at my arms either.

"It was that bar fink in the Cote d'Or," Fay said when they let us go.

So I wasn't going much to the Cote d'Or. I thought twice about going there.

Jody was past caring. *Sometimes.* I found it difficult to distinguish between her and my own projections and caught myself from time to time accepting her mask of bravado at its face value. And yet I knew that she, like the rest of us, was not always impregnable. I suppose there was a contradiction in my own desire. I found myself attracted by her pose of outrageous independence. At the same time I did not anticipate she would expect me to take it seriously all of the time.

I wanted to say: "Look, Jody, I understand. I too have a mirror." But somehow I couldn't get through to her. I said instead: "You're beautiful, Jody. I don't know how you can be with those stinking innards of yours, but you are."

Someone said she was a whore.

"Me too," I said. "I couldn't have anything to do with a woman who didn't know she was a whore. I couldn't connect for long with a woman who wasn't conscious of having been, at one time or another, a whore."

The fact that Jody did turn a trick now and again, when it was necessary, and that at the same time she didn't think of opening a shop, endeared her to me.

At hustling her fats she was the best and the worst.

She drew young Jewish businessmen like a magnet iron-filings, but they soon found out she was a sleepwalking whore, and they got uneasy and often indignant when they found out she used heroin. "Man," Jody said, "can you imagine me lettin them screw me if I wasn't high on somethin?" In itself heroin doesn't lead to prostitution. But for many women it does make tolerable the nightly outrage inflicted on them by what are for the most part spiritually thwarted men.

Moreover, Jody didn't always turn up for a date. This unreliability was attributed to the fact that she was a drug fiend by her indignant customers. And, of course, if she had been hung up without bread and with no junk she would probably have turned up to get the money for a fix. Which confirmed for those gentlemen that the best things in life cost money.

Men were always asking Jody to marry them. They wanted to protect her, to save her from herself. Many of them were rich and at least one was very rich. But what she wanted was a john who would send his check each week from the North Pole, one she could love at a distance for being so generous, while she got down to the business of loving one of her own (un)troubled kind. At all times I sensed a great capacity for love in Jody. As, I suppose, her (other) johns did.

For us to be together was difficult, at least until I went

on the scows again. I met her during a period when I had quit, when I was sleeping wherever I could find a bed. By the time I went back on the scows it was too late. She was too strung out. I no longer cared enough to make the effort. I wanted a woman who could sometimes be casual, even about heroin.

During those few months there were several ways we might have made it together. We could have stopped using junk. She could have hustled for us. Or we could have boosted from department stores. Or pushed.

Most male addicts are eventually pimps, boosters, or pushers. We made the motions of kicking. Jody couldn't bring herself to get out of bed. That was the scene that inspired Moira to say: "Jody! She just uses you! She's like a bird, a fat, greedy little bird waiting for you to come back to the nest to feed her. How much do you want this time?" I couldn't get through to Moira either so I returned to the room where Jody lay nursing her general outrage, compounding her spite, in the single bed which she hogged. As soon as I entered she accused me of forgetting the cakes.

"What cakes?"

"The cakes I asked you to get for me! The Twinkies!" she screamed. "I told you to bring two packages of Twinkies!"

"Two packages of Twinkies. . . ." Repeating it to control my exasperation.

It lasted four days and then Jody turned a trick and we got high. A couple of times and I got fed up hanging around all night diners, waiting.

We could have boosted. Most junkies we knew did that eventually. They had to to keep up their habit. But at the point at which one decides to make it as a booster one has already faced up to the probability of spending a large part of one's life in an iron cage. No doubt a man can adapt, even to periodic incarcerations. And the world will certainly look doubly beautiful each time one returns to the street. But for myself I couldn't have chosen that life any more than I could have chosen to live out most of my existence in Greenland. There is infinite possibility everywhere, up until the moment of dying, even in the skin of a leper wielding the power of his bell, but the extremity, the violence, and the sudden nature of the transitions in the existence of the inveterate convict, a life, as it were, of continual shock therapy, of brutalization, the daily endurance of machinelike discipline imposed from without, the mob and lynch-law of the numbered men, guarded by men vaguely resembling themselves in whatever "big house" of men, the daily insults, the small indignities, the constant clang of steel and glare of artificial light, eat, sleep, defecate, the daily struggle to escape the limit of one's perceptions—the Baron de Charlus, chained naked to the iron bed in Room 14A at Jupien's, was still master of his destiny in a sense in which no convict is—it would have been improbable for me to choose all that.

As for pushing the stuff, we never seriously considered that. To do it properly you have to make it your profession, and as a profession, with the vague, arbitrary, and ambiguous alliances along the boring way, it stinks.

Jody and I stayed together a few days longer until that

moment we had both anticipated when we parted somewhere near Sheridan Square, she to return to Pat's, I . . .
I don't remember.

Jody moved ahead into the bar. Moe, Trixie catatonic
under goofballs, Sasha, the White Russian, lushed, at the
brink of tears; avoid them.

"Jody!" A small woman, nearing fifty, with brown
hair, leaned out from between two men at a table in the
rear. It was Edna.

Jody nodded to her uncertainly.

"I wonder if she's got any bread?" she whispered to me.
I shook my head.

The woman made a sign, gesticulating with her fingers.
It might have meant anything. Jody shook her head to
show she hadn't understood and when Edna began to
gesticulate more vigorously Jody turned away with a
short sharp shake of the head. "Let's get out of here," she
said.

Outside again we hesitated in the drizzling rain.

We crossed the avenue and went into the drugstore
which sells the paperbacks. "We gotta get some loot!"
Jody whispered urgently when she saw I was about to
examine the books.

"Sure," I said. "But I don't know how yet."

"There must be someone. . . ."

"There he is! Wait here," I said to her.

Alan Dunn, a man I had known in Paris and who owed

me a favour, had just entered the drugstore. It was a break.
I knew he would lend me some money.

"Hullo, Alan."

"Hi, Joe! It's good to see you, man! I heard you were
here and tried to look you up. I saw Moira the other day
and she said you were working on the river. Getting much
writing done?"

"A fair amount," I said cautiously. But I knew Dunn too
well to feel obliged to mention it again. I brightened at
the thought and said: "Listen, Alan, I need some money,
now, tonight. . . ."

"Sure, Joe . . . how much do you need?"

"Twenty dollars would do."

He already had his wallet out. He handed me two tens.

"How about a coffee?" he said as I accepted the money.

"Let's," I said. "And thanks for the loot, Alan. I appreciate it."

"O.K. boy, any time," he said.

"Excuse me a moment," I said to him. I walked over to
Jody. "I'll meet you in a quarter of an hour in Jim Moore's.
See if you can set something up."

"How much?"

"Depends what it is. I got twenty."

Her smile was beatific. "We could go round to Lou's.
I'll phone him now."

"O.K. See you." I returned to Alan who was sitting at
the counter.

"Who's the girl?" he said when I sat down beside him.

"Her name's Jody."

"She's got beautiful eyes. But she looks beat. Are you living with her?"

"No. I once thought it might be nice to fall in love with her. But it wouldn't. It'd be like loving Goneril." I sipped my coffee. "When did you get back?"

"Just a week ago."

I was glad to see him. I liked to talk about France. Soon we were laughing about how *l'Histoire d'O* had been banned in Paris at the same time as it was awarded a literary prize. In Paris the corruption of literary censorship is a war the wise have waged against the foolish for centuries.

"It's good to see you, Joe!"

"It's good to see you, Alan! Where are you staying?"

He gave me his address.

"Have you heard from that Arab friend of yours? . . . what was his name? . . . ."

"Midhou," I said. We had taken Alan by bus to Auber-villiers where we knew a Spanish place. It was hidden away in the Spanish slum of Paris near a canal. It was to this district that those who were not poets came over the Pyrenees after the Spanish Civil War.

Midhou was a great smoker of hashish, a troubadour, an Algerian in Paris who ate with his hands. Seated cross-legged on the floor, the snarl of his lips emphasized by his Mexican moustache, he made his hands upwards into claws and spoke of flesh. The heavy brow, the receding fore-head, the small, pointed ears, the black eyes of a bird of prey, the foreign words spat from clenched teeth, the claw becoming a fist, becoming a knife, becoming a hand.

"Yeah, I heard he went to Algeria," Alan said.

"I got one postcard," I said. "But I heard indirectly he lost half his face driving a truck into a brick wall in Algiers. There was a police road block. I don't know whether he was carrying guns or hashish."

"Poor guy," Alan said. "Is he all right now?"

"I heard he was. I heard he was back in Paris for a while and was the same as ever. Do you remember his guitar?"

We were talking excitedly when Jody came back.

"You comin, Joe?"

"Sure. This is Alan Dunn . . . Jody Mann."

Jody nodded and Alan smiled at her.

"I won't keep you," Alan said, standing up.

"Yeah, Joe, come on," Jody said.

"I'll give you a ring," I said to him.

"And finish that book," he said.

When we were outside Jody said: "What kept you so long?"

"Fuck you," I said.

"Lou's waitin!" she said.

"Did you hear what he said to me?"

"No. Who? Lou?"

"No, not Lou. The guy we just robbed."

"Oh, him? No. What did he say?"

"He said to me: 'Get that book written.' "

"What book?" Jody said.

"Man, *any* book!" I said.

"Yeah!"

"As though that were my fucking *raison d'être!*"

"Your what?"

"I mean I didn't say to him: 'Get that soap sold,' did I?"

"Yeah man, he was too much! Lou said to hurry."

"What happened?" I said, exasperated.

"Fay's making the run. She'll be back by the time we get there."

"Who put up the loot?"

"Lou. He's puttin up ten for us."

The count we got for the dime wasn't much. Lou had poured out the shit on to a mirror and was dividing it with a razorblade when we arrived. There was Fay, and Harriet, Lou's wife, who was making a bottle for the baby, Willie, everybody's parasite, who when his personal needs were met was a man of good will, thirty-five, with bad brown teeth and thick-lensed spectacles, Lou, Jody, and myself. Geo arrived almost immediately with Mona. He was looking hot and red in the face above his white collar. He usually wore a white collar when he was with Mona. She was wearing a hat and had had her hair permed and looked like someone's maiden aunt, incongruous in her tweed costume beside Fay who had taken off her fur coat and was rolling up the sleeve of her shapeless green dress, and Harriet, her hair in rats' tails, wearing her shirt and jeans, and dangling her baby on one arm. When Geo went out with Mona he adopted a mock sanctimonious air which was to tell the rest of us he knew she was fattish, with newly permed hair and a hat she wore indoors. He explained her saying she had an ass he could get a good grip of. But his apologies embarrassed us and only tended to make Mona exaggerate her air of respectability. Mona was all right. It was sad to see Geo turn her into an awkward plagiarism of herself.

"Where's that nickel you owe me, Geo?" Lou said from where he stood at the draining board of the sink. With Lou looking at Geo the razorblade was immobile over the little heaps of powder on the mirror.

I saw a flash of annoyance come into Fay's yellow eyes.

"Lou, put enough in that spoon for a fix for me. You can take it out of mine later," she said to him.

"Why you motherfucker!" Geo said to Lou. "I made the run. I was entitled to a third. How many fixes have I laid on you?"

"Fuck that," Fay said, nudging Lou. "The spoon. Put some in. Would you shut up for a minute, Geo?"

Lou stood at the sink, not even looking at Geo now, but down at nowhere, smiling his private smile.

"Hello Harriet, hello Joe," Mona said. We were all bunched up at the end of the room (a kind of groundfloor passage or long cellar) which was the kitchen, near the stove, near the sink. Then, as she herself wasn't going to fix, she turned her perplexed attention to some ad or other which Lou had pinned to the wall. A girl was saying to her mother: "Mom . . . couldn't you get Daddy to stay upstairs when John comes?"

"Look baby," Geo said to Fay, "you still owe me a ten dollar bag. And what about the three bucks I laid on you last night?"

"Everything he says is irrelevant," Lou said from behind his smile.

Fay grunted as she heated the spoon over the gas flame.

"All this arithmetic," Willie said, choosing sides.

"Gimme some more, Lou," Fay said. "I won't even feel this."

"Sure you will! It's a dirty spike!" Jody said.

Mona moved quietly to the other end of the room, sat down, and opened a magazine. Geo followed her unconcernedly with his eyes and then said to me: "Will you tell these motherfuckers to get off my back?"

"Man, I told you before I don't want you all coming to turn on here," Lou said to Geo. "This pad's getting too hot."

"What's that got to do with it?" Geo said, grinning. "You talk about me being irrelevant? Anyway, you turned on often enough at my pad."

"Shut up for a minute, Geo," I said. "For God's sake, Lou, if you're turning on next start cooking up."

"Yeah," Jody said, "Lou'll turn on next if Fay ever stops booting it."

Fay's thick, dark, purplish-red blood rose and fell in the eye-dropper like a column of gory mercury in a barometer. A word that failed to materialize spluttered out of the corner of her blue mouth in an outward thrust of inarticulate indignation—what? accuse Fay?—her eyelids drooping, mumbling, "not . . . sure . . . got . . . a . . . hit. . . ."

"Yeah, looks bad Fay, you're wounded," I said.

"She's going to give Lou a transfusion," Jody said.

"What's your blood type, Fay?" Lou said.

"Has anyone here got the time?" Mona said from her

end of the room. To get him off the hooks, I told Geo I would give him a taste. Inspired by that good office he performed the same for Mona, telling her it was ten past two.

"I'll give Willie a taste," Lou said.

"Don't give him much, Joe," Jody said.

Harriet took the baby's bottle out of the pot of hot water and squirted a jet of milk against her wrist to test it. The baby accepted the nipple eagerly.

"Wow! dig his habit!" Willie said.

We all shot up, except Mona. —Why don't you turn her on, Geo? "No. She doesn't *use* it," he would answer piously, as though it were self-explanatory.

Tom Tear arrived with a hurt look and tried to find out if anyone had any shit left. Only Fay had, and she explained it in a vague and unregenerate way as some stashed away from yesterday and subsequently found. I always felt Fay's was a peculiarly unvenomous treachery though she seldom took much trouble to cover her duplicities, compensating for this impertinence with the added impertinence of a ready indignation—what? accuse Fay?

I remember Mona a few hours later. You couldn't complain about her patience. Or you could complain. You could say to her: "Geo turned on an hour ago. Do you think it's a bloody virtue to be so patient?" But Mona smiled at you, about as (un)ambiguously as her namesake in the Louvre, her slightly cross-eyed smile, worried, with no condemnation in her attitude. She would probably have turned on if it hadn't been for Geo. He was like a man defending his wife against swearwords. *Doncherknowtheresladiespresent?*

Geo was saying to Lou in the manner of Tertullian: "What I mean is I don't care whether you *prove* I'm an evil mother, you're lying!" and Mona said to the room at large: "Isn't he insane?"

Harriet looked demure.

"I thought you said you didn't have any," Tom said to Fay.

Fay didn't say anything. Working silently at the sink like Dr. Jekyll brewing his potion, she had no doubt hoped to go in this her second fix unobserved. Her hand trembled as she held the match to the spoon.

"Oh man!" Tom said, seeking allies.

Fay still said nothing. She drew the liquid into the eye-dropper.

"Come on, give me a taste, Fay!"

"I'll leave you a taste in the spoon," Fay grunted.

Tom came alive in a way he sometimes did.

"Man, I knew you'd make it!" Geo jeered.

"Up yours, Geo," Tom said.

"He's right, Geo," Lou said, his eyelids fluttering momentarily as he stood swaying near the sink. "You're an impertinent mother."

"Geo, I'm going now," Mona said. "I can take a taxi so it's O.K., you needn't come. You stay if you want."

Geo looked pained. "Oh baby, can't you stay a half hour longer?"

"Sure," Mona said unhappily. "It's just that there's

nearly an hour between trains at this time of night. You know how it is."

"O.K.," Geo said, "but I'll go with you as far as the station anyway."

"The family that kicks together, sticks together," Lou said elliptically, swaying.

There was a knock at the door.

"Just a minute for Christ's sake, see who that is!" Lou said, going near the door. Tom removed the spike neatly from his vein, squirted a jet of water through it, and stashed it among the knives and forks.

"Who is it?" Lou said loudly, his shoulder against the door.

"He thinks he's Horatio defending the bridge," Geo said. "If it's the Man they'll trample him underfoot. You know the time they busted me they came in with their guns out and I'm standing there with a fucking spoon. Now, if it'd been a flame-thrower!"

"Shut your fat mouth!" Lou hissed at him in an undertone.

A voice from the outside said "Ettie!"

"It's O.K., Lou, it's Ettie," Fay said.

"Fuck Ettie!" Lou said. "This pad's becoming like Grand Central Station. I don't want the whole fucking world coming here!"

"Is Fay there?" the voice said in singsong.

"Let her in, man," Fay said. "She's probably got some shit with her."

Ettie came in.

Ettie was a thin negress who shot up ten five dollar bags a day. One time she wanted Jody and me to move in with her. Ettie pushed everything, clothes and other valuables she'd boosted, shit, her own thin chops, and speculated with the minds and bodies of her friends. "Last night I had a scene with the Man," she said to Jody and me once as she opened an oilskin pouch on the bed and disclosed half an ounce of badly adulterated heroin. "Bastid had his hand on my leg right near my own sweet self. With that I can deal. I'll show that boy!"

"She will too," Jody said to me.

"He might bite your ass," I said to Ettie.

Ettie wanted us to move in with her, the two of us; Jody could hustle again and I could be the man about the place. "Then you git all the shit you want, no hassle."

"No hustle?" Jody said drily.

"I didn't say anything about that, babydoll. What are you anyway? an idealist? You know well what you kin do, Jody. You kin manipulate those soft pink fats of yours. That's Greek."

"No kidding?" Jody said.

"Man, it's a hassle what you do," I said to Ettie, "peddling around town all day with the heat breathing down your neck."

"He kin breathe right up my vagina, dear, jist so long as he don't bust me," Ettie said.

"What's this?" Ettie said now as she came in. "I've never seen so much evil in one room. If my mother could see me now! Hi there, Jody! Are you straight?"

"Joe gave me a taste," Jody said. "But I didn't get anything. Have you got some shit on you, Ettie?"

"You think I come all the way downtown just for the ride?" Ettie turned to Lou who had locked the door behind her. "Mind if I get straight here?"

Lou hesitated. I could see his point. He might as well have opened up a shop. Finally he said: "O.K., but I want a taste."

"That might be arranged," Ettie said, and, a few moments later, after a few incredibly quick motions with spoon and eye-dropper, she was probing with the needle at her thin black thigh.

Jody leaned near her.

As Ettie withdrew the needle she looked up at Jody and said: "I know what's comin and the answer is no. First there's that nickel you owe me from last week. That's yours there, Lou." She pointed to a small heap of powder in a spoon.

Harriet, after shrugging her shoulders at Ettie's entrance, had retired to the bed where she was now lying, playing with the baby. Willie was stretched out near her.

Fay was talking urgently with Geo. Mona, now seated stiffly in an upright chair near the door, looked on disapprovingly.

"Man, I've only got a nickel," Geo was saying to Fay.

"Anyone wants anything, say so now," Ettie said.

Lou, who had just fixed again, continued to sway near the sink, the dropper with the needle on it still in his right hand.

"Aw, for God's sake, Ettie!" Jody said, "I'm gettin some bread tomorrow, honest!"

"What about her?" Fay said to Geo. She meant Mona.

Geo groaned and looked pleadingly at Mona who appeared to be at the end of her tether.

"Look, Mona, you could lay ten on me tonight, and I could give it back out of that thirty."

"I thought you were going to buy a suit?" Mona said.

"Don't forget you owe me a nickel, Geo," Lou said, swaying, his eyes closed.

"Who needs a suit?" Fay said to Tom.

I was looking at Mona. She had already taken a ten dollar bill from her purse. Geo took it and said to Fay in a hard voice: "Anyway I don't see what you're gettin so excited about. I didn't even say I'd give you a taste."

"I got her down here," Fay said.

"You got her down here," Geo mimicked.

"That's correct, she did," Ettie said and turned back to Jody. "Honey, I jist can't understand what it is you think you've got between your legs that's valuable. It's jist lyin idle and meanwhile you ain't even got a nickel to git straight with."

"Yeah, it's not so easy," Jody said. "Look, Ettie, to-morrow. . . ."

"I'm going now, Geo," Mona said.

Geo was interrupting Jody. "For Christ's sake shut up for a minute, will you?" He turned to Ettie. "How much for fifteen? a sixteenth?"

"I don't know about any sixteenth," Ettie said. "You git three five dollar bags for fifteen."

"Oh, don't come on, man!" Geo said. "I can go uptown later myself and get a full sixteenth!"

"I came downtown," Ettie said.

"That's right, Geo, she did," Fay said.

"I'm not buying any five dollar bags," Geo said. "I'll score later." He turned away from Ettie and Mona said: "I'm going now, Geo. If you want to come to the station with me you'll have to come now."

Geo hesitated and then said: "O.K., baby, I'm coming now. See you all later," he said to the rest of us.

"Hey, wait a minute, Geo," Lou said, lurching out of a comatose state. "You've got to lay that nickel on me. I need it to score."

"You really think I owe you that nickel, don't you, Lou?"

"Man, you're not impressing anyone!" Lou said.

"Come on," Fay said, "you owe him a nickel. We need it. Give it to him."

"Will you hurry up and shut that door?" Harriet called from the bed.

Mona was already outside.

Lou chuckled, his face suddenly becoming friendly. "You know, you don't always have to argue, Geo. You never win anyway."

With a look at Fay, Geo gave Lou a five dollar bill. "I don't know," he said as he went out.

"That bastid," Fay said when he was gone.

"Fuck you, Fay," Lou said, smiling at her.

"She's right," Tom said. "Sometimes Geo's too much."

"Sure," Lou said, "but he's never refused you a fix."

"He's refused me offen," Jody said contemptuously.

"An I'm refusin you now, baby," Ettie said. "Now, does anyone want to do business? I got to be at 125th in an hour."

"We'll share a bag, eh Lou?" Fay said, moving at once over to the sink.

"O.K.," Lou said, and paid Ettie. "Do you want a taste, honey?" he said to Harriet.

"Yeah, leave me a taste," she said. She was playing with the baby's fine hair. "It's just like silk," she said to Willie.

"Are you going to score, Joe?" Jody said to me.

"I'll get a bag and we'll split it," I said to her.

"Half of one of her bags is nothin," Jody said sulkily.

I didn't answer. I intended to keep a nickel so that I wouldn't be stranded on the scow.

I divided the bag in two and shot up my share. Three of us were shooting up at once, each working silently and efficiently. Somehow Tom got some, and Willie. As soon as I withdrew the spike Jody accepted it from me.

"You want I should call on you Friday?" Ettie said to Lou. "I'll be in the neighbourhood."

"No, man," Lou said.

"Why don't you make it across to my place?" Tom said.

"Around what time?"

"About nine."

"See you all," Ettie said, "and you, baby, you take your mother's advice," she said to Jody as she left.

Fay sat on a low chair and began to nod.

Harriet moved quietly over to the sink and Lou gave her a shot. They went back over to the bed together.

"Will you people get out of here as soon as you can?" Lou said to the rest of us.

Jody raised her hand quickly to her mouth and dropped the needle back into the waterglass.

"Where are you going now, Joe?" she said to me. "Can I come along?"

"No, baby. I'm going back to Perth Amboy."

This time I know where I am going, it is no longer the ancient night, the recent night. Now it is a game, I am going to play. I never knew how to play, till now. I longed to, but I knew it was impossible. And yet I often tried. I turned on all the lights, I took a good look all round. I began to play with what I saw. People and things asked nothing better than to play, certain animals too. All went well at first, they all came to me, pleased that someone should want to play with them. If I said, Now I need a hunchback, immediately one came running, proud as punch of his fine hunch that was going to perform. It did not occur to him that I might have to ask him to undress. But it was not long before I found myself alone, in the dark. That is why I gave up trying to play and took to myself forever shapelessness and speechlessness, incurious wondering, darkness, long stumbling with outstretched arms, hiding. Such is the earnestness from which, for nearly a century now, I have never been able to depart. From now on it will be different. I shall never do anything any more from now on but play. No, I must not begin with an exaggeration. But I shall play a great part of the time, from now on, the greater part, if I can. But perhaps I shall not succeed any better than hitherto. Perhaps as hitherto I shall find myself abandoned, in the dark, without anything to play with. Then I shall play with myself. To have been able to conceive such a plan is encouraging.

—Samuel Beckett

I always felt it was strange that the butcher Abel should be preferred to the agriculturist Cain.

Abel waxed fat and rich breeding sheep for the slaughter while Cain tilled. Cain made an offering to the Lord. Abel followed suit with his quaking fat calves. Who'd have gruel rather than a T-bone?

And soon Abel had vast herds and air-conditioned slaughterhouses and meat storehouses and meat package-plants, and there was a blight on Cain's crop. And that was called *sin*.

Cain stood and looked at the blight on his crop. And his spade was useless against it in his hand.

And it came to pass that Abel was trespassing there where Cain would carry his spade, which is where land is to be tilled and not where sheep pasture.

And Abel saw his elder brother and he was thin and

with a starved look and held the spade to no purpose in his hand. And Abel approached his brother, saying: Why don't you give up and come to work for me? I could use a good man in the slaughterhouse.

And Cain slew him.

If I say to you: "People in glass houses shouldn't throw stones," be vigilant.

I fell asleep last night over this document. When I woke up this morning around eight I found I was the last scow in a tow of four moving like a ghost-ship in fog. I say "a tow of four" because last night there were four of us. Actually I cannot even see the scow ahead of me. I know we are moving because the wrinkled brown water slides like a skin past my catwalk. I threw an empty can overboard. It bobbed in the wake of my stern for a few seconds and then, like something removed by a hand, it was out of sight. I suppose I can see in all directions for about fifteen feet. Beyond that, things become shadowy and at the same time portentous, like the long swift movement of the log which floated by a few minutes ago.

Everything is damp this morning, cigarettes, the paper on which I write, the wood with which I kindled the fire to make coffee, and the sugar. I smell my own damp smell, wood, tar, jeans that cling smoothly to my thighs.

A foghorn sounds somewhere. It is difficult to tell from which direction it comes. The water is about me and the sudden billowing yellow shapes of fog, and somewhere in it, like a signal for me alone, the foghorn sounding. The sun came up a while ago but the mist is still low on the water and no land is visible. The scow also is very low in the water.

I lay for three days at the quarry without being loaded. There is a cement strike and contractors are reluctant to stockpile stone. Approaching the quarry, the works on the green hillside are like the carcass of some gigantic grey insect glinting grey in the sun. The sun making shadows on the dock; offices, stockrooms, and the housing shaft of the long stone conveyer belts running like an endless shanty up into the excavation. The days were sunny. The work of loading went on slowly. I waited for the daily tows to arrive—the light scows began to pile up—hoping to see Geo, or Jacqueline.

Most of the time I was abstracted from it all. Sometimes I sat outside my cabin and watched the men on the dock, the loaders, the carpenters, the scowmen going to and from the company store. I felt like a Martian; slightly puzzled, fundamentally uninterested. Sometimes when I was high I watched it all with an overpowering sense of benevolence, the green valley of the river, the water grey-silver, its shimmering surface sliding away down towards Newburgh where seriously damaged scows are repaired, the little grey motor-tug pushing scows about, like a terrier pushing floating coffins, the white-helmeted loaders all looking bronzed and fat and healthy and unimaginative, working the moving lip of the stone-chute, the scows, light and loaded, ranged up in tiers against the dock, the trucks, the cranes, the pneumatic drills sounding sporadically, and an occasional explosion from the quarry at the other side of the hill; nearer, the bucket of slops hurled suddenly towards the eddying water by a shapeless-looking woman of fifty who had been screaming all morning that her man was a drunken sonofabitch, another woman, slightly drunk, older or younger, occupied with a tub near a line of fluttering clothes, both of them unkempt, tough, ignorant, angry,—involving myself in a daydream of white buttocks striking savagely against the wooden sideboards of a bunk. Fuck, fuck, fuck, fuck, fuck. . . . Those unbeautiful women could still be beautiful in their lust . . . or could they? Currrrrump—attention distracted by a distant explosion from the hillside quarry. Then both women were gone, and a loader, six-foot-four is standing in his white helmet, light blue shirt, and dungarees, his large red hands on his hips, watching me. I nod to him. His grimace is not particularly friendly.

"You bastards sure get it easy!" he said.

"Yeah, it's a way of life."

I was wondering whether he was going to get over his resentment. I was wearing nothing but a pair of shorts and I was relaxing in the sun with a cigarette and a can of beer. My feet were dirty. I hadn't shaved for three days. He looked disgusted. Perhaps he didn't like to think of men like me existing in the same world as the wafer-white and odourless flesh of his teenage daughter.

"You bums's not supposed to drink on board, you know that?"

"Fuck you," I said.

"What did you say?"

"Ug mug tug dug," I said.

"You trying to be funny?"

I drank some beer. "You want to start a war, is that it?"

"Maybe I do," he said. He hesitated, spat, turned away. "You bastards sure get it easy," he said as he went.

The loader originally dislikes the scowman because the scowman doesn't work. That makes the job unpleasant from time to time, finding oneself having suddenly to deal with the animosity of a man who makes a virtue of his work. It is difficult to explain to the underprivileged that play is more serious than work.

So I was glad when they finally loaded me and I joined the tow going downriver again. The sun still shone and I spent most of my time lying on the roof of my shack under a sky which streamed sunlight down on to the twelve scows of the tow. The bank on either side rose steeply up from the water's edge, brown masses of bald rock grown in and over by trees. It is an historic part of America, this stretch of the Hudson, from Manhattan to Albany. The trees were very green. The scowmen were sitting at the sterns of their scows, on the roofs of their shacks mostly, watching, on chairs, like admirals on the aftercastles of galleons. Some had their women with them, on deckchairs, under gaudy beach umbrellas. And everything was very relaxed and peaceful until we passed under the George Washington Bridge.

At Pier 72 I had no opportunity to go ashore. A tug was already standing by to pull me out. That was last night. And this morning when I awoke there was the fog. They loaded me with 1½″ stone. Good and bad. Not so much dust so they don't use so much water and it comes aboard drier than smaller stuff. The stone comes down the hillside to the river's edge from the stockpiles near the quarry on a narrow canvas conveyer belt about two feet wide. The grey tubelike housing shaft high enough for men to walk in contains the mechanism of the conveyer belt. From a distance it has the distinctness of a grey arrow pointing sharply from the hilltop to the water, and, as I said before, with the other constructions might be the carcass of a grey lizard or insect. It is an el-train for crushed stone. A man in a pillbox high over the water's edge at the end of the housing shaft controls the flow of stone, gravel, or dust, which moves down a metal chute on to the scow. The smaller the stuff the more water they use to control dust. When it is dust that is being loaded it comes aboard the scow like a flood. This can be a pain in the ass. The water leaks through the wooden planks of the deck into the massive boomed bilges for hours after loading and it has to be pumped out. A deck scow carries its whole load on deck. What would be the hold in a ship is simply a heavily beamed compartment to insure buoyancy. After loading this is a dark, dripping, slimy place, murkier than under the darkest pier. I sometimes stash my spike down there in an airtight box, below water level. The trouble with 1½″ is that it doesn't usually go as quickly as smaller stuff at the unloading yards of the various sand and stone corporations, so that it is likely that one will be hung up for days without overtime, waiting to be unloaded.

I was thinking about this coming down river and I am thinking of it now, somewhere in Long Island Sound, isolated from all things by fog.

—*What the hell am I doing here?*

Why am I not in India, or Japan, or the moon?

Everything changes; everything remains the same.

—*What the hell am I doing here?*

I arrived in London the night before I sailed for America.

I decided not to look anyone up. It would have meant explanations . . . just passing through on my way from nowhere to nowhere.

I left the railway station and mingled with the other people on the street. It was the rush hour. Shops were closing. People swarmed in the dusk towards the underground. Men, small bent men, were selling newspapers. As usual I felt myself overcome by the cheerful sense of orderliness Londoners seem to exude. At times it had amused, at times infuriated me, and once or twice during the war, I remember, the sense of solidarity it implied gladdened me. This time, however, leaving France for no good reason, on my way to America for no good reason, with an acute feeling of being an exile wherever I went, I found it oppressive. I was heavy with the sense of my own detachment.

And that had been with me for as long as I could remember, gaining in intensity at each new impertinence of
the external world with which I signed no contract when
I was ejected bloodily from my mother's warm womb.
I developed early a horror of all groups, particularly those
which without further ado claimed the right to subsume
all my acts under certain normative designations in terms
of which they would reward or punish me. I could feel
no loyalty to anything so abstract as a state or so symbolic
as a sovereign. And I could feel nothing but outrage at a
system in which, by virtue of my father's name and fortune, I found myself from the beginning so shockingly
underprivileged. What shocked me most as I grew up was
not the fact that things were as they were, and with a
tendency to petrify, but that others had the impertinence
to assume that I would forbear to react violently against
them.

At that moment I found myself standing in the middle
of moving traffic, hesitating, unable to go forward or back,
clutching bag and raincoat, until the signal changed. Finally I reached the far side and moved quickly into the
crowd on the other pavement. From time to time in just
that way my absent-mindedness startled me. Although I
was walking quickly I had no idea where I was going. I had
thought about it on the boat journey from Calais to Dover,
wondering what had moved me to take a ship from Southampton which I could have boarded as easily at Le Havre.
For some reason or other I had wanted to spend the last
night in London. I had no desire to see anyone in particular. I had been careful to keep the fact of my arrival to

myself. I remember feeling a sense of nostalgia for this
national metropolis in which I had seldom spent more than
a few days. When I first visited it at the age of seventeen
I remember thinking I would one day live there, but after
years abroad on the Continent I wasn't so sure. Somehow
or other I found it difficult to take the English seriously.
I had often been appalled by the absurd contrast between
what they said and their manner of saying it, between a
frequent lack of talent and imagination and the degree of
respect they hoped to exact by virtue simply of acquiring
a particular accent.

When I say that I loved London I mean it was a place
I recognized as one in which it would be possible for a man
like me to live, where people in spite of their many ab-
surdities tended to respect an individual's privacy, to a
limited degree, to be sure, but more so than in say: Mos-
cow, New York, Peking. (I was feeling already that when
I returned from America it would be via London-Paris.)
I am not saying that Londoners are not inquisitive. They
may be more so than either Russians or Americans for all
I know, but they are a conservative people, like most people who are not desperate, and the hard core of constitu-
tional law governing the status of the individual in society
is not likely to die overnight. In London policemen do not
carry guns in their everyday business.

It had begun to rain. The streets and the grey buildings
around Victoria depressed me. I had many memories of
Victoria Station. During the war I had arrived and de-
parted from Victoria many times and the streets and
buildings round about were quite familiar. I remembered

seeing Gill's Stations of the Cross in Westminster Cathedral, refusing a prostitute who offered to masturbate me
in one of the air-raid shelters opposite the station, going
with a prostitute to one of the streets nearby and thinking
she might be older than my mother, the railway bar, the
tearooms cloudy with steam from huge tea-urns and coffee
pots, and dusty at the same time, and the dry sandwiches
under glass, the long tiled lavatories with their shifting
men, and the rush of commuters with bowler hats and umbrellas in the early morning.

It was after six o'clock; fifteen hours in London before
the boat-train; time to get drunk and sober up, to eat two
meals, to go to bed with someone. Plenty of time, and at
the same time short, like a bee's visit to a flower, and no
commitments.

I took a taxi and told the driver to take me to Piccadilly
Circus which was central enough and where I knew I
could find a room easily in one of the big hotels which
corresponded to the anonymity of my visit . . . no questions, all the necessities, all visitors passing through. Across
broad carpets to the lift, silently upwards to the nth floor,
along a corridor, realizing they had given me a room in the
rear which would open on to an airshaft and wishing now
I had asked specifically for one which opened on to the
street, the key in the lock, the door thrown open and the
light switch on, the room looking blankly as it always
was and would be, impervious to the stream of human
beings who had come and gone, the neatly made bed, the
bedlight now being switched off and on by the porter to
indicate where it was, vague hotel noises from the airshaft,

the smiling face . . . "All right, sir?"—tipped, gone, the door closed silently behind him. I squashed my cigarette in the ashtray on the glass-topped table beside the bed, protect it against cigarette burns; lay on the bed and looked up at the white ceiling at the centre of which was a small, vaguely noticeable grill. It occurred to me that it might be used to house a camera or a microphone or to inject a poison pellet to fill the room with gas.

When I had taken a shower I left the hotel again and made my way on foot into Soho where I dined at a small French restaurant. Walking down Charing Cross Road afterwards I experienced a pleasant glow from the wine I had drunk. At Leicester Square I hesitated. I wondered whether after all I should have contacted someone. What to do now? For the moment I didn't feel like drinking any more and it was still relatively early. I was vaguely regretting having come to London instead of going directly to Le Havre. If I had done so I would already have been aboard. The ship had probably docked by this time at Southampton. But what the hell, what did it matter? A man should be able to waste time without being seized with anxiety.

The rain was falling steadily, making the streets glisten. A taxi raising little streams of water at its wheels turned the corner in front of me and moved towards the bright lights at the busy part of the square. I hesitated a moment longer and then followed after it. —See a film, might as well. There was nothing else to do.

I entered the cinema and went straight to the cloakroom. The girl took my raincoat and hung it on a peg. The cloth

of her uniform was shiny; big buttocks of a red mare. She
returned unsmiling with the coat-check. I walked over the
pearl-grey carpet towards the three crimson usherettes
who stood with chromium-plated flashlights before the
swing doors of the auditorium, big, tight-skirted girls with
golden buttons and neat pageboy caps. Two brunettes, one
blonde. The smaller of the brunettes tore my ticket in half
and guided me down the aisle with her flashlight. I passed
in front of seven pairs of knees to my seat. A man with
glasses and thin pale hair sat on my left. The girl on my
right glanced at me and then back at the screen as I sat
down. She was about twenty-two. On the screen were
depicted some Asians and a flame-thrower and some burning corpses, grilled guerrillas, five hundred of them according to the commentator, being flushed from their nest.
I glanced beyond the girl. The old woman at the far side
of her was obviously not with her. She was putting a sweet
into her mouth. When I glanced back across the profile
of the girl to the screen a stick of bombs seemed to slip
from the gaping belly of a bomber and the camera tilted
downward towards the eruption. Smoke and amorphous-
ness. The commentator said that according to the latest
communiqué the mopping up phase of the battle was over
and a big push could be expected soon. The news ended
with a close-up of H.M. the Queen in the uniform of
Colonel of the Coldstream Guards. A cartoon in techni-
colour came on to the screen. It was as though a weight
were suddenly lifted from the audience. The girl beside
me moved her leg. In the faint glimmer of coloured light
her naked ankles were very pale. As the colours within the

beam shifted the paleness was tinted with green and the
skin seemed to move. The alcohol had made me feel warm
and outgoing, and I experienced a vague lust. It was pleasant to imagine her amazing white arse and the very soft
skin of the insides of her thighs. She would speak over-
correctly as many English girls do, at least until I got my
fingers between her legs, and then she would be hotter
than hell, as many English girls become when they are
groped, and possibly clumsy, probably, and I remembered
Charlie's observing in retrospect how much cleaner all
French women were about the cunt than English women
(girls), Anglo-Saxon women generally, how a French
woman's vitals would be sweet to the taste, while with
those of an Englishwoman one risked being confronted
with a holy sepulchre, a repository for relics, as in an altar,
forged somewhere in the gas-inhabited foundry of the
girl's unconscious, under centuries of propriety, if I took
his meaning. Not that he wished to make a value judgment. Not him. Tastes differed. Look at Henri Quatre of
France, who advised his mistresses three weeks beforehand
to omit their ablutions. The cat on the screen had just received the lower part of a window on the back of its neck
and was seeing stars. The mighty mouse was stepping
backwards with his hands on his hips into a trap which
was sibilantly reflected in one of the stars the cat with one
evil eye saw. A charming housewife, entering the room
as though she expected it to delight her, saw the plight
of the mouse and saved him in the nick of time. Having
done so she espied the suffering cat. She tapped her high-
heeled toe and moved menacingly towards him where he

was staggering about, recovering, and with the rolling pin she happened to be carrying near her pretty apron she struck the cat a 90° blow on top of the skull, causing him to fold up like a concertina, and, as like a spring he opened, she belted him one on the kidneys and sent him through a splintering window and by the neck into a neat crotch of branches in a tree. The narrator left us there in the daze of the starry-eyed cat. As the silk drapes moved majestically across the massive screen a multicoloured Wurlitzer rose like a whale from the sea, and the organist, rising with it in white tie and tails, drew from it a few spectacular bars of Rachmaninoff before falling into the enthusiastic melody of *I want to be happy.* . . . When he had run through that he took a bow and announced that he wanted the audience to accompany him with the words. This promised to be very painful indeed. I remembered it was the practice for it to go on for about ten minutes with the words of the songs and the beats projected on the screen and I looked quickly at the girl at my side. No visible discomfort. She appeared to be interested in the distant stalls in all directions. I debated for a moment whether or not to offer her my opera glasses and decided against it. See the film, go to bed. I would have a couple of drinks at the hotel and go to sleep easily. I didn't really want her. A cunt was a cunt, and she could be little more for me in the short time at my disposal. I began to repress all movements which might have elicited a response on her part. Not now. Not again. Early in the morning I was leaving London for Southampton and New York. And although from the moment I had arrived at Victoria I had been overcome by a sense of isolation, from time to time almost nauseous in intensity, and though it was to kill time I had entered the cinema, I couldn't at that moment face getting to know another human being, or rather, not getting to know another human being . . . at best it had been like the perfect correlation of Leibniz's clocks. Stopped by my own exaggeration I sat through the main feature and left immediately after it. Walking back to the hotel I was accosted by a woman as I turned into a side-street. I apologised and as I moved away she offered to lower her price; she asked me what I could afford. I couldn't think of anything to say and walked on in the rain back to the hotel.

Through the swing doors and into the vast reception hall. It was like a burned out world; in the stale atmosphere the hanging smells of cigarette smoke, ash, the lingering scents of women and men, all pale and in its dimmed brightness empty, a Romanesque Cathedral with a fitted carpet, lined near the street with model display windows of dressmakers, perfumeries, and haberdashers, all dimly and discreetly lit at that hour which was the very witching hour of night. A few night porters stood about, a liftman, the night clerk behind his desk talking to a full-bodied young woman in a black dress, heavily made up in the manner of managerial assistants in large, commercial hotels. Everyone seemed to be talking in whispers as though a funeral cortège were about to descend the main stairway. I crossed the hall to the lounge where drinks were served after hours to residents only. That is one of the privileges of being a registered guest in a London hotel. A number of provincial businessmen were still scattered about the lounge, talking with intense gesticulations over late drinks. The apple-green basketchairs were shabby at that hour and the lounge smells were similar to those in the hall. A vague pantry smell emanated from the green-baize-covered swing door through which the waitresses came and went. One of them, a tired powdered woman of about sixty with a blue wen on her cheek and wearing a faded black dress, served me. Afterwards, she stood at a short distance with her empty tray, her old face twisted in concentration as with the fixed and hypocritically innocent smirk of the eavesdropper she overheard the conversation between three commercial travellers from the North. It occurred to me that they, unlike me, were in London for a reason, and I began to think of the voyage.

I had travelled so often and in so many directions that I was bored at the mere thought of it. Moreover, this particular voyage had a more than usually sinister aspect; not only was I unable to produce for myself a convincing reason for going to the United States, I was tolerably certain there wasn't one; no reason, that is, other than the fact that neither could I find one for remaining in Paris, nor for going anywhere else. On previous voyages I had at least gone through the motions of satisfying myself that I should go here or there, even if the journey were for its own sake like a trip to Spain for the bullfights; but in this instance I had no means of knowing what my experience would be. And as a man was not a piece of litmus paper to register this or that property of the objective world—even as litmus paper was finally expended with too much immersion—I was sceptical of the value of going to another new place and facing an entirely new set of objective conditions. I would notice them effectively or I wouldn't. If I did, I might widen my experience without deepening it. In travel, as in all things, there is a law of diminishing returns. And if I didn't, my experience might be drastically short.

During the last year in Paris I had drifted away from my former acquaintances. I could no longer share a common purpose with them. I had spent most of that year in a small room in Montparnasse, going from it to play pinball or to distract myself with a woman. This room had three sides and one large studio window which looked out over the projecting roof of basement studios on to a high grey wall which cut off all view of the sky and of the summer sun. It was like living in the box in the kitchen in Glasgow when I was a child. I spent more and more time in the room. I can remember lying on my back on the bed, staring at the ceiling, thinking of Beckett, and saying aloud for my own edification: "Why go out when you have a bed and a floor and a sink and a window and a table and a chair and many other things here in this very room? After all, you're not a collector. . . ."

It was in that room I had begun to write *Cain's Book*, the notes for which took up a disproportionate amount of space in my only suitcase, and which I was carrying to America with me.

"Another drink, sir?" The waitress was speaking to me. The commercial travellers were getting up from their table.

"Yes please."

"That was Scorch and water, wasn't it?"

"Yes, it was."

At a certain age, looking back over the past, I began to wonder how much, except in a purely negative way when they presented themselves as limits, objective conditions really affected me. Certainly, for as long as I could remember, I had been selective of what was external to me, and not merely, I think, in the sense that all perception is selective; sometimes, and unconsciously, I had excluded "facts" with which every one of my immediate acquaintance was familiar, facts which I should consciously have judged to be vital to my own well-being if I had been aware of them. For example, in the two instances in which I had lived with women in a full-hearted way, it was a friend who drew my attention to the fact that my wife had deserted me six months ago. I remembered saying: "No, you're wrong, man. She's coming back," and then suddenly realising that she wasn't, couldn't come back, because in a dimly conscious way I had been organizing my life to exclude her, from the moment she had left me. And yet I was not quite wrong, because what was left out of the present situation as described by my friend was my own will, which, it startled me to see, he left quite out of account. And then I realized that in presenting myself as up till that time unconscious of my wife's desertion of me I had all the time demanded of him that he should ignore my will, which he saw very well, as something external to him, and fairly predictable. My momentary annoyance that he should think of me as predictable he perhaps excused in me as my friend, at the same time excusing himself, no doubt, for excusing me who he knew stood in no dire need of excuse, since nothing is predictable which is not externalized.

Sitting there in the deserted lounge reminded me of the smokeroom in downtown Glasgow where my father used to sit and while away the long hours of the afternoon. I thought that my father would be alone now, that he would have turned on the light in his room . . . it was nearly midnight . . . and would be alone. The last time I had seen him was at the funeral of my uncle who, running after a tramcar, was suddenly on his knees, arms akimbo as his heart burst.

The coffin had brass fittings and smelt of varnish. It was supported by scrubbed deal wood tressles in the middle of the parlour, and it dominated the room as an altar dominates a small church, the wine curtains pillars, and over it all was the smell of flowers and death and varnish—like the smell of pine cones—which set the mourners at a distance from the dead man far more utterly than his mere dying had. The smell pervaded the whole house, met one at the door, and as the mourners arrived in their white collars and black ties, shaking their hands, talking in hushed tones, nodding to others distantly known, it had descended on them, crystallizing their emotion, and drawn them inexorably towards the room given over to death.

I watched from a distance as the coffin was lowered into

the grave, tilting, from silk cords, and then, following the
example of the others, I threw some sod on the lid of the
coffin, a flat hollow sound from distended fingers, rain on
canvas, a chuckle of despair. Afterwards, the mourners
moved back into groups and the clergyman led a prayer;
a small man with a bald head who had donned his trappings
at the graveside, and when, without music, he broke nervously with his small voice into the 121st Psalm and the
mourners took it up, their voices ineffectually suspended
like a wind-thinned pennant between earth and sky, I
glanced directly at my father and for a moment we seemed
to understand one another. My father dropped his eyes
first, involuntarily, and I looked beyond the mourners
across the green slope where the grey and white grave-
stones, sunk in the sod at all angles, jutted upwards like
broken teeth.

After the prayers and the singing the two workmen
moved forward self-consciously and threw the earth back
into the grave, and the long block of raised earth was
covered with wreaths. "That's ours," my father said out
of the side of his mouth at me quietly. "The one with the
tulips . . ." and, feeling himself overheard by a sterner
gentleman at the other side of the family, coughed his little
cough, and said: "Yeeeeees. I believe that's it," and he was
suddenly looking at it with an almost pained expression on
his face, offensive thing, that at the beginning had de-
lighted him . . . until amongst the others suddenly he
had seen it small and less prepossessing than he had remembered. The clergyman shook hands with the family,
with Tina, whose goitre was bad and whose eyes had had

a fixed, unaligned look for some weeks, with Angus who was blinking at the first day he had seen during seven years on the nightshift, with Hector more solemn than I had known him—Tina must have been later, for of course, being a woman, she wouldn't be at the graveside— the clergyman, muttering comforts that sounded like apologies, went with his little leather case alone down the path without looking back.

The sobriety of Hector's air caught my attention. Since he had become a commercial traveller he had adopted a permanently spoofing air, a professional light-heartedness which deserted him now. But then his father was interred and he seemed to take hold of himself and to notice me for the first time. How was I? Were things going well? Lucky devil to live abroad these days! Why, the taxes in this country were past belief! Overhearty, evasive . . . this the boy I had carried on my back over a dangerous ledge near Ben Nevis. Was it not funny how everything had turned out differently, not as one expected? I had a vague idea he was referring to my clothes, informal, beginning to be threadbare—poor old Joe, gone the way of his father! My general air of anonymity.

"Come and see us before you go," Hector said, but he was already looking over my shoulder where one of his associates was buttonholing his boss. "Don't forget now, old man. Vivian and I would love to hear all about your travels, always talking about you. Marco Polo, eh? What wouldn't I give to be in your shoes!"

"Next time," my father said when we were alone at last, "it will be for me."

"Nonsense. And I shan't stay away so long this time, Dad."

I thought then it was hardly a lie; there was no way of knowing.

We lingered long after the other mourners were gone, walking along the gravel footpaths between the graves, and the grave of my uncle with its covering of bright wreaths was nearly out of sight.

"Your mother was buried here," my father said. "Would you like to see the grave?"

"Not particularly."

"You've never visited it."

"No, I never have. Would you like a drink?"

"It's just as you wish," he said, not looking at me, "but I thought as we were here anyway."

"I don't want to see it, Dad. I have explained it to you before."

Springtime, I remember thinking. To be in England. Casually I stooped to pick up a broken flower which had fallen on the path. It was quite fresh.

"From a wreath," my father said.

We walked slowly, in silence, and the sky was low and whitegrey like milk which has stood for a long time in a cat's saucer, collecting dust, and as I looked up I felt a raindrop on my face. "Looks as though it's going to rain," I said.

"I come here every month," my father was saying. "Sometimes I miss a month, but not often. It's the least I can do."

I repressed the impulse to say something harsh. I glanced at him but he avoided my eye and there was a faint flush on his cheeks. It was as though my father had said: "I'm old now, Joe, you must understand," said that and not the other thing, which was not important and which was not really what he had meant to say. I wanted to put my arm round him and say: "We're like one another, Dad," but I couldn't make the gesture.

He was looking at me uncertainly.

"I've sometimes wondered, Joe, why you haven't done something serious, you know, like Hector or your brother-in-law."

"Have you?"

"You could be independent today."

"I *am* independent."

"Of course, I know," he said. "But you know what I mean, Joe."

"Money?"

Coughing. "And position, you know. Take Hector; he's in a fine position now. He's worked hard that boy."

"You envy him?"

"Who? Me?"

His laugh was forced. I looked away at an urn on a pillar of white marble; the inscription was in Latin . . . *in vitam aeternam*. . . .

"You know that's not true, son."

"I don't want to talk about Hector, Dad. Poor guy with his infinite quotas."

"It's just as you wish, Joe. I didn't mean to upset you.

Only you were close when you were kids. Follow the
leader it was when you were boys. He followed you everywhere."

"Yes, I remember."

I wanted simply to change the subject which bored me
but my father had crumpled and his mouth had fallen. I
had an impulse to explain myself to him . . . that I would
not have had it otherwise, at no point would I have gone
back on the past . . . didn't he see? But he would not
have understood. "We're alike, Son, you and I." He might
have said that. His son, after all. The second generation.

"I realize of course," he said at last, "that I haven't been
much help to you."

The irrelevance shocked me. He would always believe
that; my son, my world; at least he could claim guilt.

I found myself saying, somewhat drily: "You needn't
blame yourself, Dad," and I was going to add: "You didn't
decide me one way or the other," but the defensive smile
of disbelief was already there, like a vizor over the eyes.

We walked on.

And then I noticed that my father's hat seemed too big
for him. It was. It didn't fit him. I took his arm:

"Your hat's too big for you, Dad!"

He laughed. "Can't afford another, Joe! D'you know,
when I bought my first hat they cost 12/6d . . . the best
mind you. The same hat costs 62/6d today. Money's not
worth what it was as Hector was saying only a few days
ago. The cheap hats are no good, no good at all. This is
a Borsalino."

A Borsalino. He had halted, removed his hat, and pointed with his finger at the discoloured silk lining. "Borsalino. Made in Italy. You see?"

"Must be a good one."

"The best," my father said.

We were walking towards the main gate of the cemetery. The cortège had already broken up and the last of the cars was gone. The porter at the gate nodded to us as we walked out on to the street.

"I suppose those shops do good business," I said to my father, referring to the row of shops which sold graveside ornaments and flowers.

"Capital," he replied. "I bought a vase there once for your grandmother's grave but one day when I went back somebody had broken it. That's a long time ago now, of course. Must be twenty years."

"And shells," I said.

"Yes, you can buy shells with inscriptions."

"Eternity in shells," I said. But my father was looking straight ahead and walking quickly as he always did on the street, and he seemed to have forgotten what we were talking about.

"Will you go abroad again immediately?"

"I suppose so. There's nothing for me here at the moment. I may spend a day or two in London."

"And then where? France?"

"North Africa perhaps."

"Was there during the first war," he said mechanically, "Alexandria."

"Yes."

"I know! It was the day before your Aunt Eleanor died."

"What was?"

"The day I found the vase broken. Sheer vandalism."

"Yes, it was a pity."

"I paid 17/6d for it. It wasn't cheap. Come on, we'll get a drink across the road there." And we crossed the street to a greenpainted public house.

It was easy there with a glass of whiskey in front of us to recreate the surface intimacy which, years before, I had assented to during a game of billiards—never pot your opponent's ball—our having even then little to talk about and our inexpertness at the game causing us to smile, to laugh, to be together, until, in the sun again, we took leave of each other, I to go to some class or other at the university, my father to drink coffee in his favourite smokeroom and to read and reread the local paper.

My father, like my uncle, used to talk about his memories of Cairo, Jaffa—the oranges were tremendous, like small melons—and Suez, to speak of a head wound he had received, shrapnel—fingering the scalp tenderly—which had resulted in his being "sent down the line" to the base hospital and thence home to Blighty, and, as he uttered the word lovingly I used to wonder how he could have failed to relate the homecoming to those things to which he *came* home—or did he come home?—for it seemed to me that those years and those vague memories were the only positive thing in his entire life—he invariably returned to them after a few drinks—and that from the day he had set foot again in England he had known nothing but humiliation. I was brought up in a world in which we could refer to my father's unemployment only in a discreet whisper and never in the presence of guests. Those were the days, Joe! You were too young of course! Good Scotch, what was it? 7/6d a bottle, yes! Jaffa oranges, pick them off the trees, get a nigger to do it for you for an acker, the price of secondhand furniture, too bad you're not setting up house, I know where you could get some cheap, know a dealer, Silverstein, good business in the East End, trust the Jews, see a man was convicted at the Old Bailey, *fif*teen thousand gold watches, that's smuggling! no wonder, income tax, bloody robbers . . . conversations which in the end always came to his noting that someone had died, to his search in the deaths' column, as though the printed notices informed him, quietly bringing desolation to his eyes, that time was running out.

I sat for a long time thinking of my father in the lounge of the hotel where, to discourage late drinkers, most of the lights had been turned out. Everyone else had gone, except the one with the wen, and even she went away for long periods, through the pantry door. But I had begun to enjoy its bleakness and its emptiness.

The murderer entered and sat down some distance away at the only other table at which a light was burning. I noticed him come in at the moment at which he entered, but it was as though I retained the visual image of his entering in a preconscious state and at a distance from what I was at the instant experiencing, the image of him flat and without contour, there during all those ten minutes during which I was still following the hollow recesses of the room into their tawdry elaboration in the mind of a professional plasterer, amongst shadows, in the oblong gloom of the ceiling, and its emptiness, and its dank, ash-laden smell, the spirals of blue smoke all ascended to a dripping unstable cloud under the roof, as in an auditorium deserted after a performance. Then suddenly—I say ten minutes—I was aware of him seated at the table under the light, like a man waiting, as he was, a white blob of a face and a dark blue suit, and I had a sense that he was elderly.

The wen came and went to his table a moment later. It might have been she who called my attention to him. I had felt her restlessness and the fact of there being another customer seemed to enliven her. And it let me off a hook.

And then we were both sitting in all that emptiness and it occurred to me that if one of us wished to speak he would have to call out at the top of his voice. If I called out at the top of my voice, officials would come from all directions, porters, nightclerks, chambermaids, to witness the taking of the madman. But it wasn't so. When the gentleman spoke, he did so in a high voice but not loudly.

"Stranger in town?"

I had not expected him to address me and was caught off guard. I began to say yes but it trailed away into an anonymous gesture of the hand which was to indicate the enormity of the room, the impracticality of carrying on an intelligent conversation at that great distance. He got up and came across. Sit here, no need to shout, he conveyed to me, and I found myself smiling acceptance. —He is now here by your explicit request, I was thinking. Anything that happens now is your own doing. The table, the man, the dim light, the wen in the pantry stealing cakes. He was about to say something but I dropped my right hand to his thigh, near the crotch, and looked him in the eye. He looked like a stunned fish, a big cod splayed chin flat on the marble. He goggled. Then he pulled himself up, struggling to remove my hand which clung to the fat of his thigh like a hook to beef, and a sly, wheedling expression was suddenly jammed close to my own, an expression which flashed intelligence of the pantry where the wen might walk. "Not here!" he said in a breathless whisper.

It occurred to me that if at that moment I were to lick his face as a cow might he would certainly scream.

When I got up to go to my room he was still at his table (which, of course, he had never left). I crossed the hall to the foyer and went outside into the street where there was a light rain. A night in London, I was thinking. Well, for Christ's sake go to bed, you don't have to write it!

"**C**apacity for love?" Geo said. "I don't know anything about that. I have noticed Jody has a capacity for horse."

Mona was trying to get a job in Indo-China and the very thought of being in that country gave Geo wet dreams. I was hoping she would get it. She was on the scows only at weekends, like some other women who had jobs during the week. As they are still employable they are usually better looking.

Mona said to me: "I'm not a kid any longer, Joe. I'm thirty-two. I know Geo can't give up horse, not now anyway, but I want to know where I stand. I don't care whether he's a good painter or not. He doesn't paint. He hasn't painted for over a year now. But I want to know if he wants me to be his woman. He doesn't live on what he makes on the scow. He's always in debt and he doesn't notice how much he's really getting from me. I don't mean only money, Joe," etc.

What are you going to say to Mona?

"She's great," Geo said, "like she's not small. I can get a good grip on her ass . . . but sometimes I feel like young, untired pussy."

There's not much young pussy in sight today. Hatless women with bare pink legs in broken shoes, red, flat, suspicious faces. But in the strong sun and the glint of the silvery water everything is at peace. Occasionally a man calls out to someone on another scow. The water laps gently at the bilges and moves back, bubbling. A small red and black tug with a large white C painted on its funnel hoots and moves away from the side of a scow and quickly towards the head of the tow. The scows are four abreast in seven tiers. Some of them have roof-gardens, a kind of window-box in which one can sit in the midst of geraniums. A circular came with our last paycheck: "Captains desiring geraniums please notify paymaster at the New York Office immediately."

The green trees; the fragrance of the trees in the water-travelled wind avoided the nostril that twitched to find a word to express it. The hairs of the earth's body; to get beyond the abstraction it was necessary to sink or soar, and that was wordless, my sitting there in the summer wind, sinking, soaring. But then my mind came back, like a scythe, to reap the corn, to refine the sensual elisions. From the tropisms of vegetables, my ancestors, no exit except through symbol, the scaffoldings of imagination. An indignity for a man to be a tree which knows other trees sexually but not women.

I was sitting, stripped to the waist in the sun, the light river wind like a cool feather at my skin, my thighs prickling on the painted wood seat, the sweat there at the loins in my shorts, smelling my own summer smell and the tar smell of the scow, a hanging warmly about my belly of summer air, and a consciousness of the hairs at my crotch in prickling sweat. I was smelling the trees and the summer air, conscious of knowing the instant of living in the summer afternoon. A moment ago, lust, with an elation behind my nose and eyes, twitched like a blade of grass at my scrotum, and my gaze came to rest on a fat woman under a beach umbrella perched hugely in the foreground of distant hills . . . put a pillow under it dear and I'll ram it home. Between the big knees and the big arse, thighs, God-given and gratefully accepted, the luscious seedy melon-slice of Eve, greedy for get, and to beget. She had red hair.

My mother had red hair. That worried me. Her body was creamy and varicose-veined at the legs. The thought of a red sex worried me. It was incongruous, almost occult . . . a single item of uncorrelatable evidence dis-

turbing my general picture of her, pointing to a vast and
formless hinterland of experience which, because she was
my mother, I felt constrained to shun. I should have
needed a new language for it. I was never able to get beyond the idea of her as "my mother." And yet at a time
which I cannot in its uniqueness recall I came bursting
bloodily out from between her spread thighs, head first,
they said, as one thrown. Her goodness was legendary
and my total experience of her—"she was a gem, she was,"
Aunt Hettie said after her death—consisted in a vague
colouration of particulars within the general construct of
her sanctity. Only the mute knowledge of her constant
loving of me was vivid as the seditious thought of the red
sex. As I grew up that became a symbol whose meaning
I was unable to comprehend, always there, strange, sub-
stantial, rather horrifying. Even up to her death I did not
become aware of the woman. I realised that clearly for the
first time when I looked at her face in the coffin. The
others touched her hair. But to me it was the hair of a bad
dead doll, undertaker's colour, and I didn't know her.

And I moved out of the past back into my glance at the
woman under the umbrella who now reminded me of Ella
(why not?) whom I had picked up on the night-train from
Liverpool to London a week after I said goodbye to my
father. Only the blue nightlight was on in the crowded
compartment and I felt her belly and thighs under a spread

coat. When we arrived at Victoria we took a taxi to where she lived in Notting Hill Gate. I remember being conscious of the fact that I was looking at the upper half of a naked woman. She was in the bed with the bedclothes drawn up far enough to obscure her navel. Half an hour before, she had got up. The soles of her feet made a flat thocking sound on the floor. In an upright position her big belly piled itself up on its own ripple just above her crinkly black pubic hairs. Her fat thighs trembled with the shock of her step. I watched them approach and pass. When she came back I met her on my knees. To see her close, her abdomen falling outwards towards my singing face, caused both me and what I was looking at to lose in separateness. I underwent a kind of catharsis. I remember my eyes moving from her hips to her navel and down, the whiteness exploding softly under the pressure of lips and fingertips, the heat, the skin close, odorous, opaque, yellowish, and pitted almost like pumice-stone, a mass which lost all distinctness as it came to rest against my forehead. Her body jerked softly, nameless, absolute. I rose from her later and went to the lavatory. When I returned she was already back in the bed. I looked directly at her, my attention held by the soft wad of hair at her armpit. Except to tell me her name she scarcely spoke. Ella Forbes. I knew nothing about her. I suspected she was married. Perhaps her husband was a commercial traveller, like Hector. She carried an assortment of articles purchased in a chemist's in her large, bucket-shaped handbag. She was a Catholic. I knew that because she was wearing a rosary she didn't take off. Her nipples were corkish. I approached on my tongue, quitting her deeply indented navel to move upwards between them, and finally I contained the warm silver crucifix in my mouth. Strong white teeth and thick lips. She used numerous cosmetics. The nails of her fingers and toes were enamelled a cyclamen red. For a few hours we were able to annihilate ourselves in each other. There was no complicated syntax between us.

The man who is constantly scrapping with the world, constantly fighting the controls that circumstance and society place upon him is only fourteen years old emotionally. At fourteen, it is normal and accepted behaviour for the adolescent to rebel against control because the adolescent is "feeling his acts," testing out his new "grown-upness" against the controls that were placed upon him as a child. But when an adult rebels so violently and constantly against his environment, he is emotionally immature in that area.

How to Make your Emotions Work for You.

Dorothy C. Finkelor Ph.D.

foreword by Dale Carnegie.

Turn on all the lights and take a good look round. Look
at Jennie in Paris drinking a cognac at the bar of the Dôme.
A few moments ago you noticed her extract her large black
tits from her wide brassière and lay them on the copper
bar. There they lie like overgrown eggplants on a tray of
burnished gold, and with them she defies the room. Jennie
is wearing a wig. She is black and fat and nearing thirty-
five and killing herself more or less purposively with drink.
Back in the room at Montparnasse she says: "Honey, I'm
not really so fat. I'm just well-developed."

"You're fat and you've got a fat black ass."

"Don't say that!"

"Goddammit, you blonde blue-eyed nymphet! Will
you open your legs?"

Feeling under your own belly the hard bristles of hers.

"Ugh." Her nostrils tightening.

"Because two farts maketh no poem, dost think two
bellies cannot?"

Jennie is always raped.

The taste of her still in your mouth. She is dressing in
front of the mirror over the wash-basin. Fuck over, dress
quick, is her experience. She seldom exhibits her nakedness,
except in defiance, in public places.

   I was like she was, hot, see? a fat lovable little boy with
an eye that peeped at her with sheer joy, the slicks, flats,
elastic tensions at her great thighs, the torque of her hot
delta which smoked a Turkish cigarette for me to see
she was all lips and hips at the base of the green pod she
burgeoned downwards from like a butter bean. As she

moved, her belly dangling like an egg on poach, she scissored her legs cleverly, and spat out the roach, which I raised to my lips. I was like she was, and she at her ease, and ripe was she as a thumb pressed on a Camembert cheese, her chevron gamey-dark like good game as she came on me and retrieved her cigarette which, like a flutist, she laid at her mouth, inhaled, and threw it away, before she leaned against me, like a sea.

It occurred to me often that to be a user in New York was to lay oneself open to a whole system of threats, not only legal; for my mind always came back as I looked down at the little heap of whitish powder to wonder what an analyst would find there. The horse is cut with all manner of adulterous powders, until, at the average user's end, there remains 3% heroin. You can usually count on 3%. But there are times when codeine or even a barbiturate is substituted for the real thing . . . so long as they stun you, they calculate. And so you look to cop again, at once, and so it goes on. To administer an overdose a pusher has only substantially to raise the percentage of heroin in what he gives you. When you turn blue your friends try to bring you round and if they cannot they discuss how to have your body discovered elsewhere, away from their pad so as not to bring the heat on them. An occasional corpse is found in a parking lot.

I look back on all the moving from city to city and across continents. Sometimes a move was to another bed,

to another room, and then suddenly, like an unguided
missile, I travelled a thousand miles. I remember travelling
with Midhou third class on a third class Greek steamer
from Genoa to Piraeus with a vague plan to meet up with
a girl who had flown to Athens, and to walk to China. We
were confined amongst cattle and other livestock to the
bows, sailing across the Aegean to the Corinth canal. At
the table in the dining-room there was Midhou, the Algerian without a country, and this old Orthodox Jew, and
myself. Midhou didn't speak English and the Jew didn't
speak French, so I was in the middle. Midhou was an Arab
who couldn't bring himself to fight for anything, and certainly not for Arab nationalism. The Orthodox Jew,
bearded, in sombre clothes, glanced distastefully at
Midhou and spoke to me of the progress they were making
in Israel.

"Not like the Arabs. You wouldn't believe it, my dear
sir, how primitive they are . . . so backward, no sanita-
tion. . . ."

"*Qu'est-ce qu'il dit?*" Midhou said to me.

"He says you're unsanitary."

"*Merde! Petit con!*"

The Jew nodded his head to confirm his own thoughts
when he saw Midhou's leer. At the first meal he discovered
that the cooking wasn't kosher. For the rest of the voyage
he ate apples and sardines and hard-boiled eggs while
Midhou, three feet away, gnawed dripping bones.

All the women in third class were pregnant.

The notes from Athens were pretty much the same as
notes from elsewhere:

For a long time I have suspected there is no way out.
I can do nothing I am not. I have been living destruc-
tively towards the writer in me for some time, guiltily
conscious of doing so all along, cf. the critical justifica-
tion in terms of the objective death of an historical tradition: a decadent at a tremendous turning point in history, constitutionally incapable of turning with it as a
writer, I am living my personal Dada. In all of this there
is a terrible emotional smear. The steel of the logic has
daily to be strengthened to contain the volcanic element
within. It grows daily more hard to contain. I am a kind
of bomb.

In three weeks in Athens I have been unable to sum-
mon the energy to climb 260 feet to the summit of the
Acropolis to see the Parthenon.

To lose my identity as a writer is to lose all social
identity. I can choose no other any more than I can
seriously sustain that. I am being left with a subjective
identity, something I am discovering (or not) in the act
of becoming.

At times I am living at the tips of my senses. I am near
flesh, blood, hair. I brood on the bodies of women, on
the red slit of the cunt opening amongst hairs, on the
pale round belly, on hot, faintly smelling thighs.

A few notes about the hot, restless streets, but not really
much about Athens. I found it more and more difficult to
get outside my own skull.

So America wasn't really very different from anywhere else when I finally arrived. A question of degree.

> Breast culture
> Land of mothers' sons
> For cunt
> Use deodorunt
> For pricks
> Kleenix

That much I couldn't go back on, and a great deal more besides.

I remember sailing into the Hudson River for the first time, on a troop ship. My first view of the Statue of Liberty, and then being amongst them, the high buildings, like matchboxes open and shut. I had seen photographs of them, walked streets in the cinema, and, armoured by Hollywood and Aldous Huxley against experience—he was a boyhood hero of mine, and I'm glad to see him on drugs at last—was consigned to the care of the indignant, and I came and went, in fear, trembling, and security, like a zombie.

During the years in Paris I had my doubts about those who had nothing good to say about America just as I had my doubts about those who talked about Europe's being dead. They were like my father and his pal who always talked about the good old days. As a child I used to think that adults when they spoke always gave the impression that one lost something by still being alive and that all places had been better in former times. Before I ever went there I heard that Paris was dead, and later I heard that Greenwich Village was dead . . . but I never found any place dead where a number of men and women for whatever reason tried to strike permanently against uncreative work. In those places I found dissent, sedition, personal risk. And there I learned to explore and modify my great contempt.

Coming to New York for the second time I came to see Moira who was right or wrong about Jody or who was simply concerned for me. When Moira left me to go to America I suppose I wanted her to go. After that I was with no other woman for long. Her image always came to me when I was with another woman, so that I was aware of something of myself fatally withheld, a corrosive element, which infected my passion with irony. I came to America not because I identified this something with the ghost of Moira—I don't suppose she would ever have left if she hadn't felt I withheld something even from her—but because the doubt which affected me came clothed in her image, the memory of her obscuring the more impalpable and graver ghost. I made the journey to have done with the prevarication.

There was more than a year's experience we had lived apart, more than a year during which I had lived even more precariously than we had done together in Paris and during which, Moira, in America, hadn't. The apparent change in her attitude disconcerted me.

"What are your plans?"

"Plans?" On shipboard I had felt like a flood victim marooned on a raft.

"I mean you can't stay here, not permanently," Moira said.

"Couldn't we eat first?"

"I'm sorry, Joe. Of course we can! I didn't mean to be like this . . . I wanted you to come . . . I really did . . . we'll worry about all that later, in a week or two when you decide what you're going to do. . . ."

Moira had met me at the boat but had gone back to work leaving me to go alone to her apartment. Waiting for her to come, fingering the objects that had been ours when we were together in Paris, playing with the Siamese cat we bought in a pet shop on the Champs Elysées, I wondered at her returning to work. It had all happened so quickly at the taxi that I hadn't, with all the confusion at disembarkation, had the opportunity to question her about it. It was only when I got to the apartment that I began to wonder. It wasn't exactly anger I felt, it was a kind of frustration, almost disgust. I had travelled three thousand

miles and Moira couldn't take the afternoon off. I went
out for a drink, walking for the first time in my life down
Bleeker Street which many friends in Paris had spoken of.
By the time she came home I had decided I was being un-
reasonable. After all, we were no longer lovers. What did
I know about her affairs? She had her own life to live.

I looked at her now and said: "What made you go back
to work this afternoon? It must have been nearly four by
the time you got there."

"I have a job. I have to earn my living," Moira said in
the voice an adult sometimes adopts to answer a child.

I know now that she had a more cogent reason. She was
demonstrating to someone that she was no longer involved
with me. But I didn't know that then. "Fuck work," I said,
bringing us to the edge of an old difference.

"You'll find New York different, Joe," Moira said,
nervously lighting a cigarette.

Watching the little scowl on her face as it bunched forwards towards the match, I felt exasperation. Her pro-
prietory tone as she spoke of New York struck me as
ludicrous and angered me at the same time. She had already
deprived me of my welcome, and now she was excluding
me from the city. And yet I felt sure she didn't intend to
wound me.

"I mean it's not like Paris," she went on, and behind the
familiar top-heavy voice I sensed her uneasiness. "Some of
the things we used to think. . . ."

"I don't want to hear your recantations. I haven't
changed."

It was becoming dark in the small apartment. Moira

reached over and turned on a small table lamp. I got up and stared uncertainly out of the window which gave on to a small yard. I could still make out the silhouette of an old-fashioned water-tower over one of the buildings a few blocks away. The tinge of blue in the twilight gave it an enchanted look.

"Moira, do you remember the view from the little *chambre de bonne* near Bastille?"

"Yes, I do," she said. "But, Joe, I *have* changed. It makes me mad to think of all those Americans in Paris always talking against America."

"What do you expect them to talk against, Egypt?"

"You know what I mean!"

"Yes, I know. But as a foreigner I didn't get the impression that they were anti-American nor that they were always talking against America. And when they did it was usually an understandable reaction to the ugly monolithic mug that America was turning towards the rest of the world at this or that particular time; they, as Americans, wanted Europeans to know that all Americans didn't have the same attitude. I hope they were right."

"They were bums! All they did was talk!"

"Some of them talked in French," I said wearily, "and anyway, you don't have to study in Paris. It's a liberal education just to be there. Moira, I wonder if you ever thought about what I think."

"I don't want to argue, Joe. We'll go out and eat. I'm sorry about today. We'll go out and eat. We'll probably meet some people you know."

"Oh? Has another flying saucer arrived?"

For a man of imagination, of tentative will, it is not simple to adapt to the rude government of modern times. Extreme predicaments, if I do not bore the reader with such a frivolous topic, call for extreme measures of adaptation, significantly at an individual level. Hymns to democracy will not eliminate human differences, or will do so only when they incite murder, and then at our peril. After all the cant, *I* am the ground of all existence. God said it. Say it after him. All great art, and today all great artlessness, must appear extreme to the mass of men, as we know them today. It springs from the anguish of great souls. From the souls of men not formed, but deformed in factories whose inspiration is pelf. It is a kind of transcendence, it involves expression, and a symbolic object; the latter by the way. The critics who call upon the lost and the beat generations to come home, who use the dead to club the living, write prettily about anguish because to them it is an historical phenomenon and not a pain in the arse. But it is pain in the arse and we wonder at the impertinence of governments, which by my own experience and that of my father and his father before him have consistently done everything in their power to make individuals treat the world situation lightly, that they should frown on the violence of my imagination—which is a sensitive, responsive instrument— and set their damn police on me who has not stirred from this room for fifteen years except to cop shit. . . .

The Way of the Black One is crooked and full of a Curse! Ayeeh! Ayeeh! Og, escaped from the ordeal of the Bitter Waters, and come through Thunder and Lightning to Sheridan Square, took shelter under a Traffic Light, under lancing Blue Rain which washed away the left leg of his Abominable Trousers, leaving him *exposed*. Nevertheless, Og, a man of Experience, to whom both Mandala and Chaos were as an Open Book, and who had felt upon his Lewd Lip divers Nymphets with the Intimacie of a Moustache, hoped in his present disguise as a Tibetan Prayer Wheel to pass still for an Innocent Pedestrian. To distract his attention from the Fact of his Inadequate Shelter, he practised a Surprised Smile and shifted his Dirty Spike from his Crotch to his Surgically Elongated Nostril. Fuzz ran to Arsehole too frequently these days, he reflected, caressing the Innocent Nostril with the smell of his Bad Balls.

Fink saw him where he stood, turning his Prayer Wheel and leering with Assumed Innocence at bystanders. Fink's Toothless Lower Jaw cupped his stubbly Upper Lip like a Treacly Spoon or Hot Snatch and he pressed himself like a Rampant Fungus to the Wall.

Fay's Blue Thighs trembling under her Black Fur Coat were aware of themselves all the way along West 10th.

In a Nearby Cinema, Berti Lang, the Manager, was standing in the Velvet Foyer, invoking Impure Thoughts of Beryl Smellie's Bum. Berti's Wife, Chrissie, was the Cashier at the same Cinema, but she was presently in St. Vincent's having her Operation. Agnes Bane, the Senior Usherette and his wife's Informer, was at that moment out of the Cashbox where she was deputizing for Chrissie and at the Ladies' Toilet for her Evening Pee. Thus Berti was detained in the Foyer.

When Agnes returned she reported the Presence of an Undesirable Woman in the Ladies' Toilet but Berti was quite short with her much to her Astonishment. He even took off his Glasses and polished them and that as Agnes Knew was something he did only when he was hot and bothered. He left her and went like a Bent Hairpin towards the Auditorium.

Meanwhile, in the Ladies' Restroom, Fay was probing the back of her Ice-Blue Hand with her Dirty Spike. She was intent on her Bloody Work.

In the Auditorium Bertie watched Beryl Smellie where she stood in the Half-Darkness against tall red Velvet Curtains. That was how he had imagined her, a White Stain on the Red, caressed with the Body Smells and Scents of the Auditorium, and when he moved down the aisle towards her with his Official Step his penis prickled against his Miami Beach Underpants and grew hard. Close to her, Unseeing Eyes following her Profile to the Screen, he stood, and against her Fair Meat his forefinger wiggled like an Obsequious Worm.

If I let him feel my Seemly Snatch, calculated Beryl, I can get away at once, meet Fay in the Can, and split.

She did.

"Fay!" she called in the Ladies' Toilet, "Fay!"

"Dbaeioug eukuh. . . ."

"Fay!"

"Dbaeiou. . . ."

At that moment, as the door from the Foyer was pushed open to admit a Stream of Ladies, Beryl was aware of Music which signified the End of a Feature.

I had just finished my third blood-drawing, a small sketch of a schizoid white phagocyte. I thought three would be enough to constitute evidence if I were ever hauled into court for marks. I doubted if the Supreme Court would go along with the impertinent counsel that a man should not be allowed to draw his own blood for the purpose of painting pictures.

When all other means fail me I employ
a mechanical device.

It's not far from Flushing to the Village. There's a train as far as 42nd Street, but again I won't go in. There's nothing for me to go there for now. It is as if plague struck my shadow city . . . and the rest fled. Only the citadel remains, for those who aren't behind bars.

The citadel, centre everywhere, circumference nowhere; lethal dose variable. It happens to many that they can no longer go outside the citadel. For one reason or another.

I remember nights without, cold streets, unfriendly saloons, great distances. Fear. Nine hours until daylight (not that that made much difference, except that you can sit in the park amongst people who play), no reason for being anywhere rather than anywhere else, and without. (There is no one in this city before whom I can weep.) Noticing things like traffic signals and lights in porches and on empty lots; the failure to notice would bring back the reality of being without the citadel. The alien city. The hostile faces. The bars blared and the automobiles were particularly like space-ships. A corner drugstore opened its crocodile jaws and exhaled yellow light. Four crooked figures set wide apart at the counter, four men, and a stand of bright paperbacks. (The dispensary, like the vault of the old lady of Threadneedle Street, was in the rear.) Walk along 8th Street after midnight and feel the men lean towards you. —Some other time my dears, some other time.

"I regret everything," I say aloud to the typewriter. And mentally I draw blinds. But I forget, or adapt, or metamorphose. The persistence of bodily process does for the resolve.

A cigarette. I operate the roller to see better what I have written:

—Alone again. I might say amen but don't or can't. My way is not the way of the Sansaras, to shake frail claws for bread and spit on women. I must walk in crowded places, until I am murdered by my own contempt. I am alone again and write it down to provide anchorage against my own mutinous winds.

Reading what I have written, now, then, I have a familiar feeling that everything I say is somehow beside the point. I am of course incapable of sustaining a simple narrative . . . with no fixed valid categories . . . not so much a line of thought as an area of experience . . . the immediate broth; I am left with a coherence of posture(s). I thrust my chair back from the table and stand up in the small wooden cabin. —Moreover, what's not beside the point is false. Two steps across the cabin to the little mirror splashed with toothpaste and the viscid remains of mosquitoes, greeting my own sudden reflection: *"N'est-ce pas,* motherfucker?"

I need a shave. A smear of soot on my right cheek. I move closer until my nose is almost touching the glass and stare vacuously at the pupils of my eyes.

Butter I forgot to put on ice has melted to a state of sticky semi-transparency in its soot-flecked saucer. With a movement of distaste I lift it from where it lies on a spread copy of Dahlberg's *The Sorrows of Priapus.* Something in the text catches my eye:

> According to Philo, Cain was a profligate, and all malcontents are licentious.

Cain. Third profligate, first poet-adventurer, he creased her massive centrale, moved his carcassonne through her pairoknees into her soft spain before Moses engraved tablets. Not enough to lament, Jeremiah, even the decay of symbols. The butter, where to put it . . . the cabin seems abnormally cluttered up with all manner of debris, crunch,

a damn eggshell pushed gently by the toe of my boot under
the battered cast-iron coal stove . . . there. I place it carefully on a small shelf beside scissors (so that's where they
are!), jam, and insect spray; then sit down with relief and
look again at the paper in the typewriter.

—The trouble with me, I reflect, is that I look pruriently
over my own shoulder as I write and I'm all the time aware
it's reality and not literature I'm engaged in.

I press the tabulator, to sluice away my uncertainty, and
begin to type:

—An old man called Molloy or Malone walked across
country. When he was tired he lay down and when it
rained he decided to turn over and receive it on his back.
The rain washed the name right out of him.

It's a question of making an inventory. This afternoon
I stood in the yard of the Mac Asphalt and Construction
Corporation and felt like making an inventory of the
things and relations that are near me now.

—*Cain's Book:* that was the title I chose years ago in
Paris for my work in progress, in regress, my little voyage
in the art of digression. It's a dead cert the frontal attack
is obsolete.

And it's not the first time I've felt like making an inventory. (A little Lucifer constantly discovering himself after
his eviction.) I have tried more than once. Everything I
have written is a kind of inventorizing. I don't expect ever
to be able to do much more, and the inventories will always

be unfinished. The most I can do is to die like Malone with a last dot of lead pinched between forefinger and thumb, writing perhaps: *Mais tout de même on se justifie mal, tout de même on fait mal quand on se justifie.*

From time to time I think up epilogues for *Cain's Book*. God knows if I'll ever be able to put a stop to this habit. I would need an eye in the back of my head and a hand to propel me by the scruff of my own neck. Wanting them, and with the creeping behind, the sudden onsets of panic, the epilogues are easily explained. To fall on myself from above, like the owl on the wee grey mouse.

Outside, on the canal, a tug hoots. I get up and go outside on the catwalk, the narrow strip of deck between the door of the cabin and the stern of the barge. The small green tug moves swiftly past me and continues on its way down the canal towards the East River. The deck under me rises and falls gently with the swell.

The unloading crane has temporarily stopped work. The operator is on the dock, talking to one of the dock-hands. A light blue Ford, its large tail lights blinking red, is going through the gate of the yard on to the street.

The canal water is smooth again in the wake of the tug, a muddy grey-green colour, its dull mirror surface bearing a scum of oil, dust, paper, and an occasional plank of wood. There are two yellow sand-scows at the yard at the other side of the canal. The scow which is nearly light looms over the loaded scow like a pier over a low-lying jetty.

On the light scow which will be pulled out with the tide
is a Portuguese negro and his woman and his dog. The
cabin of the other scow is locked up.

Earlier in the afternoon I sat outside on the catwalk and
watched the negro who stood watching his scow being
unloaded. The crane over there has a distinctive putter.
Even across the short breadth of the canal it seems to come
from a great distance, like the sound of a tractor in a field
far away, and that sound mingled with the sound of all the
other cranes working on the canal, and they swung about,
the grabs rising and falling, hawsers straining, and they
were like big steel birds with no wings and no plumage,
nodding and pecking all the afternoon. The man was
smoking a pipe. His woman came out of the cabin from
time to time with a bucket of slops or to hang up wet
clothes. I couldn't make out her features clearly, but she
was wearing a drab, almost colourless smock, and she was
blonde. I got the impression she was big, with heavy
buttocks and strong thighs.

Scow women are not often beautiful. The exceptions
are the transients. I never spoke to a woman who looked
forward with equanimity to dying on the scows. Women
more than men have a need for roots and the shifting barge-
life with its hard, primitive conditions breaks down a
woman's resistance. And it doesn't happen often, a
woman's dying on a scow. When it does, it is like when
Geo was lying at Newburgh and the old wino woman fell
in and got drowned, at night, and they dragged her out
with a boathook in the early morning, her clothes sodden
and her face purplish-grey. The police visited all the scows

lying there at the time to try to find out whom she had been with. No one claimed her. As Geo said, she might have been pushed in, and anyway, who was going to admit to a woman like that? He was just taking his morning fix, Geo said, when this loud knocking came on his door. A beetle in a child's tin can. He thought they had come for him, that someone had tipped them off about the heroin. By the way they knocked he knew it was the fuzz, Authority—there were three of them, one was in plain clothes, an old guy of about sixty. It was he who spoke: "Where's your woman, son?" It had taken a moment for that to register. Geo's mind was anchored to the shit and works he'd stashed quickly away in the table drawer. "Where's your woman, son? She not come back last night?" Geo is always having narrow shaves.

The only sign of life aboard now is the faint trickle of smoke from the stack above the shanty-like cabin. They're probably cooking something. It's too warm for a fire.

The operator is turning again towards the crane whose grab lies like an armoured fist on my load of gravel. I return to the cabin.

There are moments when I despair of others, give them up, let them stray out of the circle of light and definition, and they are free to come and go, bringing panic, or chaos, or joy, depending on my own mood, my state of readiness. Readiness—as every Boy Scout knows—there is the virtue of the citadel.

From the bundle of papers which have withstood my periodic prunings I select a couple of sheets and read:

—The fix: a purposive spoon in the broth of experience. (*Il vous faut construire les situations.*)

To move is not difficult. The problem is: from what posture? This question of posture, of original attitude: to get at its structure one must temporarily get outside of it. Drugs provide an alternative attitude.

On the virtues of heroin. Possibility waits beyond what is fixed and known; there is no language for it; *dies zeigt sich.* . . .

Heroin is habit-forming.

Habit-forming, rabbit-forming, Babbitt-forming.

For conventional men all forms of mental derangement save drunkenness are taboo. Being familiar, alcoholism can arouse only disgust. The alcoholic humiliates himself. The man under heroin is beyond humiliation. The junkie arouses mass hysteria. (The dope fiend as the bogeyman who can be hanged in effigy and electrocuted in the flesh to calm the hysteria of the citizens.)

It is a significant measure of a society to scrutinize its sewage and abominations. Doctors know this, and police, and philosophers of history.

I remember thinking that only in America could such hysteria be. Only where the urge to conform had become a faceless president reading a meaningless speech to a huge faceless people, only where machinery had impressed its forms deep into the fibres of the human brain so as to make efficiency and the willingness to

cooperate the only flags of value, where all extrava-
gance, even of love, was condemned, and where a million faceless mind-doctors stood in long corridors in
white coats, ready to observe, adjust, shock-operate
. . . only here could such hysteria be. I thought that
there were werewolves everywhere in the wake of the
last great war, that in America they were referred to as
delinquents, a pasteurized symbol, obscuring terrible
profundities of the human soul. And I thought: Now
I know what it is to be a European and far from my
native soil. And I saw a garbage truck, one of those great
grey anonymous tanklike objects which roam the streets
of New York, move beetle-like out of 10th Street into
Sixth Avenue, and on its side was a poster which read:
"I am an American, in thought and deed." And there
was the Statue of Liberty too.

Sometimes, at low moments, I felt my thoughts were
the ravings of a man mad out of his mind to have
been placed in history at all, having to act, having to
consider; a victim of the fixed insquint. Sometimes I
thought: What a long distance history has taken me out
of my way! And then I said: Let it go, let it go, let
them all go! And inside I was intact and brittle as the
shell of an egg. I pushed them all away from me again
and I was alone, like an obscene little Buddha, looking
in.

At what point does liberty become license? And a question for the justices: *How many will hang that the distinction may crystallize?*

Whenever I glance back through the notes accumulated
over the years I am struck by their haunting sense of dis-

possession. The image of the hanged man recurs frequently. (I even went so far not long ago as to fashion a doll out of an old sack and some rope, its face greenish-grey with streaks of red and black paint, and to suspend it in a hangman's noose from the yard of the mast. It is a common practice among scowmen to fix some emblem or other to the mast. But mine was unusual. It caused too much comment, and with junk aboard I felt it prudent to remove it.) It is as though I have been writing hesitantly, against the tide, with the growing suspicion that what I have written is in some criminal sense against history, that in the end it can lead me only to the hangman.

—*Notes towards the making of the monster. . . .* That was one title I considered. At those bad moments when the dykes crumble there is a certain relief in inventing titles. On one scrap of paper I find the following notation: *In its lust after extinction the human soul has learned promiscuous ways.* I can't remember when I wrote it nor to what precisely it referred. The notes are not consecutive; they go on and on, like tapeworm; Cain's testament, the product of those moments when I feel impelled to outflank my deep desire to be silent, to say nothing, expose nothing.

When I write I have trouble with my tenses. Where I *was* tomorrow *is* where I *am* today, where I *would be* yesterday. I have a horror of committing fraud. It is all very difficult, the past even more than the future, for the latter is at least probable, calculable, while the former is beyond the range of experiment. The past is always a lie, clung to by an odour of ancestors. It is important from the beginning to treat such things lightly. As the ghosts rise upwards over the grave wall, I recoffin them neatly, and bury them.

It is, I suppose, my last will and testament, although in so far as I have choice in the matter I shall not be dying for a long time. (One can only cultivate oneself as one awaits the issue.)

If eternity were available beyond death, if I could be as certain of it as I at this moment am sure of the fix I have only to move my hand to obtain, I should in effect have achieved it already, for I should be already beyond the pitiless onslaught of time, beyond the constant disintegration of the present, beyond all the problematic struts and viaducts with which prudence seeks to bridge the chasm of anxiety, with the ability to say, avoiding unseemly haste: "I'll die tomorrow," without bothering to intend it, or not to intend it, as bravely as the fabled gladiators of ancient Rome. It is because it is not so available (—I beg of you, Abel, refrain from flaunting your faith at me) that I have to suffer the infinite degenerations of objective time . . . a past that was never past, was, is always present; a present past and a past present both distinct from the present prospect of the past degenerating already into a future prospect which will never be . . . suffer that, be prey to anxiety, nostalgia, hope. . . .

The problem has always been to fuse the fragments of eternity, more precisely, to attain from time to time the absolute serenity of timelessness; not easy in the era of pushing, aggressive democracies when all revolt not subsumed under the symbol of the juvenile delinquent tends to be regarded as either criminal or insane or both. (Revolt, my child, revolt is a quick axe cleaving dead wood in the forest, by night. The woodsman of the day is the executioner.)

A few weeks ago I tied up next to Bill's scow. There was no sign of Jake about whom I had been thinking a great deal since the night at the stake-boat. I asked him where she was and he said he didn't know, that she had gone to visit her mother in North Dakota but that he hadn't heard from her for two months. I went for a drink with Bill and I had vague thoughts about splitting from New York and going after her. I didn't suppose I would. Bill's talk about her, his saying how mixed up she was . . . all that depressed me.

Tired of the scows and of New York, my New York, the limits that make my going there from where I am tied up in Flushing at the Mac Asphalt and Construction Corporation uninteresting . . . I think, Why go? why go anywhere? . . . A familiar sound. Like the end is the beginning and vice versa. Though nothing is ending in spite of the bust which Fay comes all the way from Manhattan to tell me about:

From Tom Tear's loft you can look down on the Bowery. It is on the top floor, three flights up, of a building that appears derelict from a distance. On the ground floor, a wholesaler of cheap felts; on the first, a name painted in black on two musty frosted glass panes of two dingy doors, one at either end of the landing, O. Olsen Inc., Exterminators; on the second, a glass door boarded unevenly up, marked "Store," and this absent sculptor, Flick, who shares a w.c. with Tom. The w.c. has no door to it, but it is set slightly back from the stairs so that someone going up or downstairs won't necessarily see the occupant.

Fay saw the police go up, heard the shouts, and watched them all come down, three cops, she said, first, in uniform, called off the beat probably, and then a plainclothesman holding on to Jody's arm and talking into her ear, and then Tom with another plainclothesman, and wearing his cap ... no doubt he'd made them wait while he put it on ... and then the rest, Og, who looked like something the cat brought in, and Beryl—you must meet her, Joe—whom Fay had brought with her, and Geo, and Mona crying, he almost carried her, Fay said, and a cop bringing up the rear. There were three cars and one paddy-wagon outside on Bond Street.

"How do you know that?"

"I ast a man after," Fay said. "They was standin outside that bar, all the bums cheerin the heat on. They didn't get Ettie either. She left five minutes before they came."

Fay sat through it all, her knees bare, in her fur coat, on the w.c. between the second and third landings, amongst the spiders and the dust under the unshaded 15 watt electric light bulb, battling her chronic constipation. She didn't risk a move in case they had a man on the street but she unscrewed the bulb and sat in the dark as they came down with the others.

"It was Fink," Fay said. "He tried to bum a fix offa Geo in Sheridan Square before we all went to Tom's. Geo told him to fuck off. We shouldn't have gone there after that. But Tom had a meet with Ettie."

"How did you find out where I was?"

"I phoned your office."

"I'm glad you found me. Christ! I nearly went in last night. I could have been there!"

Fay was fiddling around in the tin basin where the dirty dishes were. She came out with a teaspoon.

"You got your works, Joe?"

I gave her the spike and dropper. "I'll leave you a taste," she said. "That creepin bastard Fink! He gets so much for what they call 'makin' a case' . . . someone's goin to slip him a hotshot. . . ."

"I'll clean it," I said, accepting the spike from her when she was finished. I tightened the tie about my arm and watched the veins rise up, a blue network in which the pale liquid would presently move like a mute caress to my brain.

In early life sensations like metaphysical burglars burst forcibly in (to) the living. In early life things strike with the magic of their existence. The creative moment comes out of the past with some of that magic unimpaired; involvement in it is impossible for an attitude of compromise. Nevertheless it is not the power to abstract that is invalid, but the unquestioning acceptance of conventional abstractions which stand in the way of raw memory, of the existential . . . all such barriers to the gradual refinement of the central nervous system.

It is not a question simply of allowing the volcano to erupt. A burnt backside is not going to help anyone. And the ovens of Auschwitz are scarcely cold. When the spirit of play dies there is only murder.

Play. *Homo ludens.*

Playing pinball for example in a café called le Grap d'Or.

—In the pinball machine an absolute and peculiar order reigns. No scepticism is possible for the man who by a series of sharp and slight dunts tries to control the machine. It became for me a ritual act, symbolizing a cosmic event. Man is serious at play. Tension, elation, frivolity, ecstasy, confirming the supra-logical nature of the human situation. Apart from jazz—probably the most vigorous and yea-saying protest of *homo ludens* in the modern world—the pinball machine seemed to me to be America's greatest contribution to culture; it rang with contemporaneity. It symbolized the rigid structural "soul" that threatened to crystallize in history, reducing man to historicity, the great mechanic monolith imposed by mass mind; it symbolized it and reduced it to nothing. The slick electric shiftings of the pinball machine, the electronic brain, the symbolical transposition of the modern Fact into the realm of play. (The distinction between the French and the American attitude towards the "tilt" ["teelt"]; in America, and England, I have been upbraided for trying to beat the mechanism by skilful tilting; in Paris, that is the whole point.)

Man is forgetting how to play. Yes, we have taught the mass that work is sacred, hard work. Now that the man of the mass is coming into his own he threatens to reimpose the belief we imposed on him. The men of no tradition "dropped into history through a trapdoor" in a short space of 150 years were never taught to play, were never told that their work was "sacred" only in the sense that it enabled their masters to play.

The beauty of cricket. The vulgarity of professionalism. The anthropological treason of those who treat culture "seriously," who think in terms of educating the mass instead of teaching man how to play. The callow, learned jackanapes who trail round art exhibitions look-

ing for they know not what in another's bright turd.
How soon Dada was mummified by its inclusion in the
histories.

Many of the poets and painters in Paris in the early
Fifties played pinball; few, unfortunately, without feel-
ings of guilt.

Art as the way, symbol, indirect, transcendence.

Her hands the texture of dried prunes—my mother used
a green block of cosmetic called "Snowfire" to take the
chapped look out of them, but they were never long
enough out of water for it to make any difference. Including the lodgers, she had to launder for twelve people,
and cook for them, and clean up their mess. It gave her
great pleasure to read about and to see pictures of the
Queen.

"What's wrong, Joe?" she said to me.

"Nothing," I replied.

Hard work never hurt anyone, I was told, but it killed
my mother.

The Industrial Revolution brought in its wake Five
Year Plans and possibly something more than lip-service
to uncreative work. My natural aversion to such work in
the land of the industrious Scot caused me, forcedly, to
dissimulate. The fact of my Italian ancestry—the name of
my great countryman, Machiavelli, was used in Scotland
almost solely as an opprobrious epithet—made the mask

inevitable. Later I whispered eagerly the words of Stephen Daedalus: "silence, exile, cunning," but at the time all that was possible was silence, cunning. Meanwhile I preferred brushing my mother's hair to make it beautiful to breaking sticks, running errands. I came closest to her at night when I brushed her hair. Alone with her in the kitchen I stood behind her chair on a box and brushed her hair until it glowed softly like burnished copper. I never knew my mother when she was young and, they said, beautiful, and sometimes when I passed my hand over her hair I was invaded by a sense of outrage that she was not young and beautiful to have me.

Whenever I contemplated our poverty and how it situated me, apparently at the edge of an uncrossable gulf at whose far side strolled those fortunate few who lived their lives in well-mannered leisure, I felt like a tent pegged down in a high wind. Sermons on the sanctity of hard work, and there were many such sermons, were offensive to me. I thought of my mother's hands, and of her poor bent body, and of her boundless admiration for the chief symbol of that class towards which all people of my acquaintance aspired, the class which did not work, the class of whose scorn my father was afraid, thinking only of money as he did, because he did not have any, because each shilling was doled out to him until he was driven to pawn the spoons Mr. Pitchimuthu from West Africa had given her as a Xmas present in—?—for getting over her shock of his eating raw eggs directly from the shell, of his frying sardines, more, expecting her to fry them for him, for accepting him black as black coal into her house and allowing him to be known as "Sir" to her children, a politeness we children never thought twice of according. To some black men. "I think I will have a yellow man next," my mother said, and in spite of my father's protest went ahead with her experiment in lodgers. I wonder now as I am suddenly overcome with the past's vast possibilities whether this could have had something to do with the citadel my father constructed in the bathroom, against comers, white, yellow, and black. My father, the Italian musician who, when he became unemployable, conducted a cold war no more (perhaps no less) idiotic than the cold war which has been going on since I was first informed men banded together in military groups. I remember one interval of seven years when groups were not at cold war, a period during which "my" group was at war. And beyond the walls of my father's house all legal precedent seemed to be governed by that class which did not work. It was true more and more of them were beginning to work, even before the Second World War, and some of them even believed that work was good for a man at the same time as they made no practical distinction between creative and mechanical work.

—"Why is work good, Mammie?"

"It wouldn't be good to play all of the time, Joe."

"I don't see why not, Mammie." Wishing as I brushed her brittle auburn-grey hair that she could play all of the time—from now on. "I don't like work."

"Yes you do, Joe."

"No I don't. I hate it. I don't like having to go to school. I wouldn't go if it wouldn't get you into trouble."

"Yes you would, Joe. You like school once you get there. It's getting up to go you don't like."

"Sometimes. I usually hate it. I hate school, Mammie."

"You learn some nice things at school, Joe."

"Mammie, why did Daddie sell the teaspoons; do you not think you should leave him for doing that?"

"No, I wouldn't leave him for doing that, Joe," and occasionally she would burst out crying and say: "If only he wouldn't be such a wild bear! If only he would leave me alone. If only he would go away and leave me alone!"

"Oh Mammie! you don't want me to go away and leave you alone? You won't go away and leave me alone, will you, Mammie!"

"No Joe! Don't be silly, darling! It's nothing . . . really! I just needed a good cry! Oh Joe. . . ."

"And I won't leave you ever, Mammie! I promise! You'll always have me!"

"One day when you're grown up and a man," she said, holding me tightly to her.

Later I said: "You don't really want Daddie to go away and not come back?"

"No, Joe, I'm all right now. You go to bed like a good boy. I'll be all right. And I'm not far away here in the kitchen."

My father came in.

"I'm going out," he said. It sounded like an ultimatum.

"You went out last night, Louis," my mother said. "I have nothing to give you."

"I didn't *ask*, did I?"

"I gave you two shillings last night."

"I didn't ask you for any bloody money!"

"Don't lose your temper, Louis."

"I'm not losing my bloody temper! I didn't ask you for any bloody money! We've never got any bloody money because you're too bloody soft on them, the whole bloody lot of them! Pitchimuthu with his bloody fried sardines and that old bloody cripple in the blue room! Kept me out of the bathroom all bloody day with their bloody carry on!"

"Louis, you just stop this! Stop it at once! Go on out if you must, but don't begin that business all over again!"

"Always defending them. They can make a bloody pig stye of the whole place! You don't care! You let'm do as they bloody well like! Well, not in this house! Not in my house they bloody well won't! I'll tell the whole bloody lot of them to get to hell out of here!"

"No you won't, Louis, you won't!"

"Do as they bloody well like! Powder all over the bloody toilet seat! The damned dirt on their feet all trod into the bloody carpet! Did you see the carpet in the bloody hall today? Can't wipe their bloody feet!"

This, then, is the beginning, a tentative organization of a sea of ambiguous experience, a provisional dyke, an opening gambit.

Ending, I should not care to estimate what has been accomplished. In terms of art and literature?—such concepts I sometimes read about, but they have nothing in intimacy with what I am doing, exposing, obscuring. Only at the end I am still sitting here, writing, with the feeling I have not even begun to say what I mean, apparently sane still, and with a sense of my freedom and responsibility, more or less cut off as I was before, with the intention as soon as I have finished this last paragraph to go into the next room and turn on. Later I shall phone those who have kindly intimated their willingness to publish the document and tell them that it is ready now, or as ready as it ever will be, and I surprise myself at feeling relieved, as I once surprised Moira at feeling relieved one New Year, knowing again that nothing is ending, and certainly not this.

New York, August 1959.